THE MAKING OF A FAST GUN

The Story of Colt McCoy

By Thompson Burnside

DORRANCE
PUBLISHING CO
EST. 1920
PITTSBURGH, PENNSYLVANIA 15238

Dorrance Publishing Co
585 Alpha Drive
Suite 103
Pittsburgh, PA 15238
Visit our website at *www. dorrancebookstore. com*

ISBN: 979-8-88729-371-4
eISBN: 979-8-88729-871-9

Life's circumstances sometimes take us in directions we never see coming. All Colt wanted to do was help his father s ranch to grow, and when the time was right, get to know the girl of his dreams. But standing up for a friend would lead to a wildfire of circumstances beyond his control. Life would take him on a ride no one would understand, a life of a fast gun.

Chapter One:

THE HICKORY TREE

Colt McCoy was the youngest of three brothers who lived on the 'Little K' ranch in east Texas. The "K" was for Kattie, his mother: his father, Dan, had bought the ranch soon after they were married and, with the help of his three boys, built a place they could be proud of on 600 acres. They ran about 300 cattle with other livestock, including a few sheep. Most cattlemen in the area, who now had learned sheep could coexist with cattle, had a few sheep for those times they got tired of eating beef. It wasn't the biggest ranch but it was a good one and they were making it pay.

It was Saturday, which meant Colt was going to town and Ethan, his oldest brother, was going courting. For the past year Ethan has been seeing June Stevens, whose father owns the General Store in Deepwater. June works with her father at the store and Ethan finally got the nerve to ask her to dinner, since then, he's been sitting with her at church and on Saturday nights on her front porch. The family sat down for dinner before the boys would head off to their adventures in town.

"I was paying the bill at the General Store today," said

Colt's father, glancing up from his dinner at Colt. "Another four boxes of . 38 caliber shells, what in the world are we doing with so many shells?" Mark, who is a couple years older than Colt, was fast to answer, "Colt's trying to chop down an old hickory tree down by the creek Pa. He's not using an ax, he's using his pistol, another 10 boxes of shells and he'll have it on the ground."

Now it's Ethan's turn, "He's been down there practicing his quickdraw against squirrels Pa, but they're not in any danger," Colt's oldest brother shoots him a glance and smiles. Colt was used to his brothers ribbing him and just laughed it off, but he 'was' practicing his draw. It started, innocently enough, one day when he drew and shot that hickory tree on a whim. But he noticed how smooth the . 38 Colt Navy revolver came out of his holster, and with practice, he was getting faster. He didn't have a desire to be known as a fast gun, but he enjoyed shooting, so every time he got the chance, he would stop and practice. He was afraid his father was about to put an end to his buying extra shells, but his father said no more about it.

"You boys go to town, but remember, there's church in the morning." It didn't matter if you were sick as a horse, there was no excuse good enough, Kattie expected her family to be in church on Sunday. "Yes Ma," the boys said in unison.

After dinner, Colt and Ethan got ready to head to town, Colt, to the Golden Lady Saloon, Ethan, to see June. Colt saddled up Rufus, his big roan, and headed west, knowing Ethan would catch up quickly, Ethan wouldn't want to be a minute late to see June. And sure enough, Colt heard the clatter of hooves coming up behind him and suddenly Ethan was riding beside at a slow gallop. They rode along in silence for a while then Ethan pulled up close. "Colt, let me ask you something." "I guess you need money to buy June some fancy perfume, how much you need?" "No, it isn't that, but it is about June though. June isn't," he hesitates. "You've seen June and I……."

Colt knows what Ethan's trying to say, June isn't the prettiest girl in Deepwater and she's a little over weight, "Listen Ethan, June's one of the prettiest girls I've ever seen. There's a lot of things that makes a girl attractive, and June's one of the nicest people I've ever met. Look how she gives food to, Whiskers and Little Joe, they would starve if it wasn't for her. She's got a big heart, and the way she helps people at the store, I've seen beautiful looking girls who were downright ugly inside. You couldn't find a better girl than June." "Thanks Colt," a few seconds pass, "Hey, Colt, about that loan," they both laugh and head to town.

Colt ties Rufus up outside the Golden Lady Saloon and goes in to get a drink. The place is already crowded so he finds a place at the bar, like he usually does, and gets a beer. He looks around and sees the poker games are already starting. Then he sees Jesse Harris and his three brothers sitting at a table in the back. Colt doesn't really have a dislike for Jesse, he just doesn't like his type, arrogant and a smart mouth. Oh, but there is one thing he likes about Jesse, and he likes it a whole lot, and that's his little sister Kay. Colt and Kay have been flirting for a long time, smiling during church or as they pass on the street when she's with her daddy. She should be turning eighteen soon so he hopes maybe then, maybe soon, it will be more than flirting.

After a few minutes, here comes Whiskers and Little Joe, two old harmless cowboys, who would rather have a drink than eat. They see Colt and come running, he always takes care of them when he's in town, whether it's a meal over at Doolin's, or a bottle. Tonight, it's a bottle all their own, they don't have to sit outside and hope someone buys them a beer, they can come in and be like everybody else and have a good time. Colt likes that, they weren't outcasts when he was around.

Suddenly, the swinging doors open and in steps Two Jacks Akers, known only as Two Jacks, and his friend Big Bob. It's rumored that Two Jacks got his name by bluffing an eastern dude holding a straight, out of a pot of over a thousand dollars, with just two jacks. Some say the dude knew if he didn't fold, he probably wouldn't live to spend the pot. Big Bob got his name because he is big, real big, about six foot six, 350 pounds. Got his reputation punching out drunks and men half his size.

They come in and head for their table, Two Jacks likes to sit with his back to the wall. The farmers sitting there take their beer and join Whiskers and Little Joe at a near-by table. It's been said that Two Jacks and Bob use Deepwater as a place to hold up in between their business ventures. Like maybe holding up a stage over in Dulles two weeks ago. The passengers said one wore a black leather hat and the other was a 'big' man. The descriptions fit perfectly but no one has the nerve to accuse them, including Marshall John Myers of Deepwater, John's been the Marshall here for 18 years and is not necessarily known for his fast gun, but Two Jacks is.

Colt has a few drinks and later sees Ethan enter the saloon and motions for him to come over, "How is June doing tonight?" "Fine, just fine, I saw Rufus still tied up out front and thought big brother would come in and have a drink with you." Colt gestures, and the bartender brings a bottle, Ethan don't care much for beer. They stand at the bar and talk for a while when they hear someone remark: "I thought I smelled something, it's sheep farmers wearing that sheep perfume," everyone busts out laughing. It's Jesse making fun of Colt and Ethan. Wesley Harris, Jesse's dad, was one of the cattlemen who refused to have sheep on their ranch and held a grudge against those that did. Colt and Ethan laugh, they can take a joke alright, but Jesse won't let it go:

"Hey Colt I hear when it's cold you like to snuggle with one of those sheep," everyone laughs. Ethan turns to face Jesse, "That's right Jesse, his favorite sheep is named Marybeth." Everyone really bursts out laughing now, they know Jesse has been sweet on Marybeth Hughes for a long time. He says she's his girl, but all that's happened is he danced with her a few times at the town dances. But now the jokes on him and he doesn't like it. Everyone continues to laugh but Jesse is on his feet heading towards Ethan. Jesse is about to learn something Colt learned a long time ago when he tried wrestling with his older brother and that's that Ethan is as strong as a bull.

Jesse reaches out with his left hand to grab Ethan by the collar, Ethan grabs Jesse by his left wrist and pulls hard, stepping out of the way, letting Jesse's belly hit the bar bending him over. Ethan quickly takes his right foot and kicks Jesse in the behind. The place explodes with laughter, Ethan grabs the bottle and moves away shouting, "Who needs a drink?"

Everyone's shouting and laughing, Jesse turns quickly and Colt puts his right hand out to hold Jesse back. "I wouldn't do that Jesse, if you're going to dish it out, learn how to take it." About that time Ethan breaks out singing a stupid song he sings all the time, good Lord, he's getting drunk, but everyone's having a great time. Colt wonders though if Jesse will let this go.
"OH, I KNOW A GIRL NAMED EILEEN"
"UGLIEST GIRL YOU EVER SEEN"
"FACE LIKE A BUFFALO"
"LEGS LIKE A SQUIRRELL"
"BUT I WANT EILEEN TO BE MY GIRL"
"ME AN EILEEN GONNA GET HITCHED"
"SHE MAY BE UGLY"
"BUT HER DADDY'S RICH"

The place erupts again with laughter, it's been a fun night, but soon Colt and Ethan start the long ride home, it's about midnight, Ethan's still singing, just not as loud now: "Oh, her daddy died last Sunday, We're getting married Monday" Then things get really quiet, and Colt knows what's coming next. Ethan has stopped and Colt rides ahead a little way, to give Ethan space to: "Blahhhhhh,

Oh God, Blahhhhh, Never again, Blahhhhhh" Colt laughs to himself, thinking, and you have to be in church in the morning.

The next morning Colt is sitting beside his mother in the pew and he can see her glance across to where Ethan is setting with June and her family. Ethan is leaning over in misery, Colt just smiles, and thinks, not singing much this morning, are you, big brother?

Then Colt glances to where he knows Kay sits every Sunday and there she is looking back, smiling. She's got light brown hair and hazel eyes, and today she's wearing an orange dress. Colt looks at her long and hard, wanting to burn into his memory what she looks like in that dress. His mother takes his hand and holds it throughout the service.

When the service is over Colt goes outside, there's a lot of people who stay afterward talking to people they only see on Sunday. Some of the men stand out front of the church talking cattle and horses. "Colt, Colt?" he turns, and it's Kay, "Drive me home?"

Colt doesn't say a word, he quickly ties Rufus to the back of her buggy, gets onboard, and turns the buggy to the east and heads for 'The Tall H Ranch'. Kay takes his arm and sits as close as she can get. Colt likes this a lot, a whole lot. They talk for a while, wondering why something like this has taken so long, of course her brothers being like they are is one good reason.

There's a grove of oak trees beside the river not far from the ranch, Colt pulls into the shade of the oaks. As soon as the buggy stops, Colt knows what he wants, he's waited for this a long time. To his surprise, Kay has the same idea, he reaches for her and pulls her close as she hugs him around his neck. Nothing has ever felt so good, he then moves in to kiss her lips that will be, more, soft and tender, then anything he will ever feel again. Her kiss is long and sweet, the only thing he can imagine that would come close to that first kiss, would be the second one, he holds her so tight he's afraid he's going to hurt her but she's squeezing tighter too. He would remember her in this orange dress and remember this kiss for the rest of his life.

Colt stopped the buggy at the sign that said The Tall H, "Is this close enough?" he asked. "Yes, thank you Colt, I hope I can see you again soon." "How about tomorrow morning, at the grove, about ten?"

"Yes, that would be great," she reaches over and kisses him gently before he gets down and unties Rufus. He would ride across the mountain to avoid running into any of the Harris family coming home from church.

Colt met with Kay twice that week and each time he comes closer to saying something that he's never said to a woman before. He's thinking about her all the time. Colt is feeding Rufus when he notices a rider approaching, it's Bud Miles, one of his best friends, "Hey Bud, how you doing? I was looking for you at the saloon Saturday."

Bud doesn't get down from his horse, something's obviously bothering him, "Colt, I have something to tell you." "Ok, what Bud?" "It's Whiskers." "What about Whiskers?" "He got hurt, really bad, Big Bob beat him up last night at the Golden Lady. I know how you feel about him and Little Joe, so I came over to tell you." "What? Big Bob beat Whiskers, why would he beat up an old man like that?"

"You know how him and Two Jacks are, always looking for trouble. Whiskers was just wanting a drink and Bob said he bumped into him and caused him to spill his. Bob grabbed him by the shirt collar and lifted him off the floor and hit him several times, it was awful Colt, just awful, Whiskers was lying there on the floor moaning and bleeding." "Ok Bud, you coming to town tonight?" "Sure, if you are." "I'm coming." Bud turns and rides away. Colt gets on Rufus and rides down to the hickory tree.

It's Saturday night and the town is busy. As he approaches The Golden Lady, Colt sees Bud in the street sur-rounded by some of the men from town. One thing about Bud, he can't draw fast, he can't hit the broad side of a barn with a bullet, but he can twirl a gun like nobody you've ever seen. It gets him a lot of drinks, he twirls it around his finger, twirls it over his head, tosses it into the air and grabs it by the barrel with his left hand, throws it back in the air grabbing it by the barrel with his right hand, flips it around, spins it around his finger and shoots in the air six times before twirling it again and putting it back in the holster. It's as good a show of gun handling that you'll ever see. The men all applaud and pat him on the back and, inevitably, someone offers to buy him a drink.

Colt ties up Rufus and walks in with the crowd. He sees Two Jacks playing poker at his usual table and Big Bob at the end of the bar. He and Bud get a beer at the bar. Some of the guys are still talking about Bud's twirling display when Big Bob opens his mouth: "I saw a girl do that in Wichita, don't take much, it's how you shoot that thing that matters, can you shoot that thing girly?"

Bud ignores Bob and he and Colt continue to drink, "My friend asked you a question sissy, can't you hear?" This time it's Two Jacks, who is standing. The card players clear out of the way, Bud steps away from the bar and takes a step toward Two Jacks, "Sure, I can hear."

Colt reaches out and stops Bud, then steps in front of him facing Two Jacks and Bob, "Listen, Colt I can handle...""You holstered an empty gun Bud," Colt explains. "What, dear God, yes I did," realizing his mistake. "I got this Bud," Colt looks at Big Bob, "You sure you want to do this, I'm not a little old man Bob?" Colt looks at two Jacks, "You can either sit down or die first, I really don't care which."

"WAIT RIGHT THERE, HOLD UP, NOBODY'S DOING ANY SHOOTING TONIGHT," It's the Marshall and his deputy

Mike, Mike is only 20 and has the deputy job because he idolizes Marshall John and listens to the Marshall's stories. Most of the time he looks lost and right now looks scared. "What's going on here?" the Marshall asks. "Nothing John," answers Bud, "Just a little misunderstanding, that's all." "Alright Bud, you and Colt clear out, this misunderstanding is over."

Colt and Bud walk outside, "My God, thanks Colt, I would have faced him with an empty gun," Bud says as he draws his gun to load it. "I've never seen you like that Colt, what were you going to do?" "I was going to kill both of them," replied Colt, climbing up on Rufus, "You better go home Bud, see ya." Bud just stands there in kind of shock, he's never heard Colt talk like that.

It was a Saturday morning two weeks later and Colt had met Kay in the oak grove. She had worn a white dress and he had to stop to look at her sitting in her buckboard in the morning sun. She was beautiful, and Colt enjoyed their meetings more and more. He couldn't get enough of her kisses and was enjoying them so much he didn't hear Jesse Harris ride up from behind until he was right there:

Colt turned quickly, "Oh, I didn't hear you." "I know you didn't," replied Jesse, "You were busy." Colt wasn't sure what to say next, it was an awkward situation. It was Kay that broke the awkwardness of the moment, "Jesse, I'm eighteen now and I can see who I want."

"Your right, I just hoped you would make better choices. Go home Kay, I need to talk with Colt, don't worry, not about you, just go home." Colt jumped down from the buggy and Kay left for home. "So, what are we going to talk about Jesse?" "You haven't been to town today, have you Colt?" "No, I came here first, why?" Jesse takes a deep breath, "Bud Miles is dead, Two Jacks killed him last night at the Golden Lady." "What? What happened?" Colt is stunned.

"Two Jacks shot him down, used the Missouri Quick Draw, it was more murder than a gun fight." The Missouri quick draw is when someone wearing two guns pretends they're going to draw with their left hand but their right hand is already on their other gun. It baits someone to go for their gun but they don't have a chance because the hand on the right gun is already drawing and firing. If you don't know what you're seeing, you think someone is lightning fast but in reality, they cheated, it's murder. "Bud couldn't win, even in a fair fight, what happened?"

"Big Bob was running his mouth to Bud all evening. Finally, Bud had enough and when he squared off with Bob, Two Jacks took over and baited him to draw, Bud never cleared leather. Thought you would want to know, and by the way, your little rendezvous, hasn't been a secret for some time now. Just making up my mind on how to handle it. Give my regards to your brother," Jesse turns and rides away.

Colt went home and didn't say a word about Bud. If he did, there was no way he would be able to go to town, and he was going to town. He left the ranch about nine, the Golden Lady would be in full swing by the time he got there. Colt rode up to the saloon and tied Rufus up out front. He stood for a second, and then walked inside:

Two Jacks is in his usual place with his back against the wall playing cards, Big Bob is in his usual place at the end of the Bar: Colt faces Two Jacks, "You murdered my friend, stand up." Two Jacks stands, "Listen boy......" "I didn't come here to listen. ...."

Two Jacks has his right hand on his pistol, ready for the Missouri Quick Draw. He moves his left hand, and as quick as lightning, Colt pulls his . 38 Navy Colt and blows Two Jacks right hand half off. Two jacks, stumbles backward and, actually sits down, in the same chair he was sitting in, screaming to high hell: "AHHHHHHHHHHHHH AHHHHHHHHHHHHHH"

Colt twirls his gun once and it's back in the holster as

fast as it came out. He turns toward Big Bob, "I'm not an old man you coward." Bob makes a move and Colt draws and fires a shot through Bob's right eye, followed by two quick shots to Bob's chest. Big Bob was dead before he hit the floor.

Colt heads straight for Two Jacks who is holding what is left of his right hand. Colt throws a couple of chairs out of the way and then the table. Colt walks right up to the screaming Two Jacks and puts the barrel of his pistol in Two Jacks mouth and pulls the trigger, blowing teeth and bone out the back of Two Jacks head and onto the wall.

He backs off, looks around, goes to the bar, throws a dollar on the bar, grabs half a bottle of whisky and turns to the door. Besides someone puking, the place is silent, until: "HOLD IT RIGHT THERE, COLT, WHAT HAPPENED HERE?" It's the Marshall and Deputy Mike. The Marshall walks over and looks at Big Bob and Two Jacks. "GIVE ME YOUR GUN COLT, WE'RE GOING OVER TO THE JAIL AND TALK ABOUT THIS."

"I'M NOT GOING ANYWHERE JOHN," Colt looks at the Marshall. "COLT, THESE MEN'S GUNS ARE STILL IN THEIR HOLSTER." "I GAVE THEM A CHANCE TO DRAW, WHAT WAS I SUPPOSED TO DO, WAIT FOR THEM TO SHOOT FIRST?" "LISTEN COLT......"

"NO, YOU LISTEN JOHN, THERE'S ENOUGH WITNESSES IN HERE TO TELL YOU WHAT HAPPENED. JUST LIKE THERE WAS ENOUGH WITNESSES TO TELL YOU WHAT HAPPENED TO BUD MILES. I BET YOU DIDN'T TAKE 'THEM' OVER TO THE JAIL TO TALK. DON'T COME IN HERE TRYING TO PUSH MORE OF YOUR LAW ON ME THAN WHAT YOU DID THEM. NOT TONIGHT, JOHN. I'M LEAVING, EITHER I'M WALKING PAST YOU, OR STEPPING OVER YOU, THE CHOICE IS YOURS."

Suddenly people start to talk, "It was a fair fight, John." "I've never seen anything like it," says another. "The fastest I've ever seen, but it was fair." "They had a, fair chance, faster than greased lightning I tell you." Colt walks out the swinging doors and throws a leg over Rufus and rides down the street. He passes Jesse Harris and his three brothers heading to the saloon, Jesse doesn't speak, Colt doesn't care.

Colt rides slowly towards home then turns down the meadow and stops at the hickory tree. He lets Rufus graze and sits with his back to the tree and takes a drink. In the early morning he hears a horse approaching and, as his eyes focus in the dawns early light, he sees the only person he wants to see right now, it's Kay. She's riding a horse with just a bridle and jumps down and runs to Colt: Colt takes her into his arms and squeezes tight, "Oh, Colt, are you alright? Jesse told us what happened, I don't know what I'd do if something happened to you." "I'm fine Kay, how did you know...." He's interrupted by exactly what he needs right now, a long soft kiss from Kay.

"I went to your house, Mark told me to look here." "Your Pa, Jesse, they won't be happy you came here, but I'm so glad you did," Colt holds her tight. He knows things could change for him now. It's not just who he killed, but how he killed them, stories like this spread like wildfire. "I guess you told Mark what happened, that's ok, better they hear it from you. I'll stay out of town for a while, let things calm down. You better go home Kay, and I will too."

Then Kay says something Colt will remember for a long time, there's a lot about Kay he will remember for a long time, "I love you, Colt." Colt cherishes, this last kiss, he doesn't know if there will ever be another one. He helps her up on her horse and watches her ride away, he's fully aware he didn't say it back.

Colt enters the house to total silence, everyone's at the breakfast table. He sits down, even though he doesn't feel like eating, takes a flapjack, but lets it lay on his plate. He doesn't look at anyone, he sits with his head down. He replays the events of the previous night in his head, he wouldn't know how to explain it even if they asked him to. Bud may have been his best friend, he did what he thought needed to be done, right or wrong.

No one says a word for the next few minutes, then everyone gets up and heads for the door, going to church. Colt stays seated, Mark puts his hand on Colt's shoulder as he passes, the family leaves, Colt sits there alone. Nothing is said about what happened over the next two weeks but Colt notices any errands that includes going to town are given to his brothers. He and Mark are working on the gate to the corral where two new mules are being kept.

Ethan rides by," Hey Mark, Ma needs you to go to Steven's for some things she said she needs today," he holds out a store list. "Awe Ethan, let Colt go, I need to finish…." he catches himself, "Oh, that's ok, I need a few things myself." Colt takes off his gloves, "Give me the list, I'll go." Ethan looks at him, "Give it here, I can't hide here on the ranch forever." Colt takes the list, hitches up the wagon, and rides towards Deepwater.

Colt notices people are looking at him a little more than usual as he rides into town. He stops the wagon in front of Steven's General Store and starts to go in, as soon as June sees him, she comes running out and hugs him, "You ok Colt?" "Sure June, I'm fine." Colt notices a stranger ride by on a big gray, he's wearing a black hat with a silver hatband that matches the silver on his holster and boots.

"We all hated what happened to Bud, his father was in here just yesterday. Everyone's been talking about how you stood up for your friend, just be careful Colt." "I will, will you fill this order June? I'm going to get a drink and I'll be right back." Colt gives the list to June and walks over to the saloon. It is Saturday, so it's a little busy, even this early, Colt stands at the bar and orders a beer.

"Are you Colt McCoy?" he hears someone ask, he turns to see a young boy to his left, the boy may be eighteen, but he looks a lot younger. Colt turns slowly to face the boy, "Yes, I am, who are you?"

The boy, wearing a pair of coveralls and a straw hat, is wearing a big gun, but his holster looks funny wrapped around those coveralls. The boy gets a funny look on his face as he sees the look on Colt's face, "OH, NO, NO, IT AINT LIKE THAT, I just wanted to meet you. My name's Billy, I'm from Stillwater. Is it true you killed Two Jacks and Big Bob, and how you killed them? Did you shoot Two Jacks in the mouth?"

"I guess so……." Colt sees the stranger he saw riding the big gray and wearing all the silver, come in the swinging doors. He stops and looks at Colt. The boy notices Colt looking past him at the stranger and about falls down getting out of the way.

"Are you the boy they say killed Two Jacks and Big Bob?" asks the stranger. Colt takes a deep breath. "They say you were defending your friend?" "That's right," Colt steps away from the bar. "What if I told you Two Jacks and Bob were my friends?" "I'd say you needed a better class of friends."

"Do you know who I am?" asks the stranger. "I don't care who you are," answers Colt. The stranger's eyes widen, then he draws, Colt draws his . 38 and shoots one, two, three, four times into the stranger's chest, dropping him to the floor with his gun still in his hand, unfired.
 Colt hears someone say, "That's Little Johnny Dawkins, he killed six men down in Allura during the range war."

"Four to the chest," says Little Joe, "Every pig farmer's son, from here to Kansas, anyone who has a gun will be coming here to make a name for himself now. They've already heard what happened from here to Tulsa and from there to Dodge, now this. You didn't bring this on yourself, but it's coming," Little Joe looks at his friend with concern.

The doors swing open and the Marshall steps over the body and looks at Colt," Is this who I think it is?" he asks. Someone tells him it is, and what happened. He shakes his head,

"Colt, you know...." "Yeah, I know Johnny, I know...." Colt walks past him and heads home.

The next morning is Sunday and Colt waits in the oak grove hoping Kay would meet him there. He doesn't know what to say to her now, things are so far out of hand. Maybe they could leave, but go where, where could he hide from all this? And it's just beginning. Colt sees two riders approaching and soon can tell it's, Wesley Harris, and Jesse, they approach but Jesse hangs back and Mr. Harris rides up to Colt:

"Colt, do you really want to bring her into this?" "Into what, Mr. Harris?" "This isn't going to end, and anyone who comes looking for you won't care who you're with, or who gets killed, including Kay. Ever since Kay's mother died, we all have sheltered her as much as we can, maybe too much. When we found out she was sweet on you, we really hadn't figured out what we were going to do, now this. I'm asking you, as her father, don't bring her into this. This is your mess, and it's going to be a mess. I know why you did what you did, but it's bigger than you now, and bigger than you and her."

Colt looks down, knowing what he says is right, and shakes his head yes. Mr. Harris rides on past headed home. Jesse rides past, "Give my regards to your brother." "What? That's the second time you've said that," Jesse keeps riding, "JESSE, JESSE, WHAT DO YOU MEAN BY.... . Jesse rides on. All Colt can think of right now is Kay, it's over.

It's been over a week and all Colt can think about is seeing Kay one more time. He wanted to tell her something, there were things that needed to be said before.... . before he did whatever it took, to make all this go away, whatever that was. He and Mark were closing the sheep up in the little corral, their father had sold them to a guy over in Dulles, they were more trouble than what they were worth. Colt notices a lone rider sitting on his horse watching from just beyond the main gate.

It was too far to make out who it was but they were just sitting there watching.

"Who's that?" asks Mark, who had noticed the rider too. "I don't know," replied Colt keeping his eyes on the stranger. "What does he want, why don't he ride on in?" "I've got a good guess," Colt says as the stranger turns his horse and starts to ride towards town, looking back over his shoulder at Colt.

"Is he here for you Colt, is this how it's gonna be, coming here to the ranch?" "I don't like it either Mark, if he wants something, I guess I better go to town and see what." "Colt, you can't keep doing this, sooner or later, someone's gonna ...." he stops, not wanting to say it.

"Yeah, sooner or later......" Colt walks to the barn to saddle Rufus.

Colt rides into Deepwater and people look at him with a look of horror on their faces. What the heck is going on? He rides slowly down the street, and then Deputy Mike runs up to him: "Go home Colt, go home now!" "What's wrong Mike, go home why?" "Frank Davis is in town and he's asking about you, go home and stay there."

Colt knows exactly who Frank Davis is- he's the most notorious gunfighter in Texas. They say he's killed 30 men or more and even if that number is mostly legend, he has killed plenty. When the kids play with their wooden guns in the street, you can always hear the name of Davis, everyone knows his name, and his reputation. He always dresses in a three-piece suit, a black hat, black boots, black holster and two pearl handled pistols. If he's asking questions, then that must have been him at the ranch.

"Thanks Mike, but I can't go home, not now. Where's your star?" "What?" "Your star, your badge, where's your badge?" "I quit Colt, I wasn't made for all this, Two Jacks, Little Johnny Dawkins, Frank Davis...... Arresting drunks on Saturday night I didn't mind, but this has gotten so out of hand, go home Colt, please," Mike turns and walks away. Before Colt can move, a crowd starts to gather, Colt looks, and walking down the middle of the street in his three-piece suit, eyes on Colt, is Frank Davis. Colt slides off rufus and ties him to a nearby post.

"Are you the boy who killed Two Jacks and Little Johnny?" asks Davis, removing his coat, folding it and hanging it over a hitching post. "Leave me alone Davis, I don't have a quarrel with you." "I didn't come here to leave you alone. You've made quite a name for yourself boy." "I'm asking you, just leave me alone."

"I can't just leave boy, the things you've done, and what I do, are things of legends. They're the things people write about, things old men talk about, young boys dream about. I can't just leave now, I was way up in Tucson when I heard what you did, I've come a long way to make history with you boy."

"Was that you at our ranch?" "Sure, it was me, I wanted you to see me." "You came to my home, around my family? Well, I saw you, and now I want you to see me......" Colt walks out to the middle of the street. "If you want to make history Frank, then make it......" Both men draw, both men shoot, Colt feels the burn of hot lead in his shoulder as he fires one, two, three times into the chest of Frank Davis, who stumbles backwards with a look of surprise on his face, and falls in the street.

The crowd stands silent, not believing what they just saw, a notorious gunfighter of legend, not shot down by the law or another notorious fast gun, but by a local boy who stood up for a friend, and through circumstances, not of his own making, will now be hounded by every fast gun the west has to offer. "Let us take you over to Doc Blanchard," Colt turns to see two friendly faces, it's Whiskers and Little Joe. He's bleeding badly from his left shoulder, as he holds on to his friends, he is lead to Dr. Blanchard's office.

Colt is up early and packing, he will wait till the family

leaves for church to avoid any goodbyes with the folks. He'll write soon and explain, but they have to know this was inevitable. His door opens, it's Mark: "Ethan didn't come home last night, Ma's worried sick." "He probably went to the saloon after seeing June and had one too many," replies Colt. "Probably fell off his horse while throwing up, he'll be along." "Well, Ma wants us to go get him." "Ok, just don't say anything about what you see here, me packing."

As Colt and Mark walk out the front door, they see Doc Blanchard's buggy approaching, followed closely by a wagon with what they can tell is Ethan's horse tied to the back. This can't be good. Doc Blanchard pulls his buggy up to the front: "Give Mike a hand there, boys, it's your brother Ethan, got himself beaten up by Jesse Harris last night."

Mark runs to the back of the wagon," What happened?" It's Mike, who explains, "Seems Ethan came into the Golden Lady last night to celebrate, he had asked June to marry him. He had a few drinks and when he was about to leave, Jesse asked him why he wasn't singing about his ugly girlfriend. Then Jesse said, I mean your ugly fiancé, Ethan went after him and Jesse cracked him over the head with his pistol."

"He'll live," says Doc Blanchard, "He's got some stitches, busted his head wide open. The Marshall asked me to wait till this morning to bring him home, he was afraid you........, well, it was late." Mark helps Mike take Ethan into the house. Colt can't believe Jesse would do this, he just couldn't let it go, being embarrassed by Ethan in the saloon.

"Thanks for patching him up, Doc," Colt says as he stares at the ground. "Colt, don't get any ideas, I know how you must feel." "You have no idea how I feel right now Doc, no idea," Colt goes into the house, grabs his packed saddlebags and walks slowly to the barn. Colt rides to the fork in the road, beyond the oak grove, leading to 'The Tall H' to wait, he sits where no one can see. He soon hears riders approaching, he steps into the road, there's four riders coming and he can tell it's Jesse and his three brothers…….

Jesse and his brothers stop, with Jesse in front, his brothers look terrified. One of them speaks to Jesse in a panic, "I told you Jesse, I told you he would come, you just wouldn't let it go." Colt looks Jesse in the eye, "Get down Jesse." Jesse stays in the saddle, "I didn't mean for it to go this far…." "Get down Jesse." "Colt, there's no need. …."

"I'm not going to tell you again, get off your horse now." "What, you come here to kill me, Colt?" "No, I didn't come here to kill you Jesse……I came here to kill all of you." "Wait a minute, Colt." "Oh, I'm gonna kill you Jesse, but I don't want to get shot in the back by one of them some dark night. I'm gonna end this here, right now, now get down or die where you sit, I really don't care."

"I can't beat you Colt…. . listen I'm sor……" "You should have thought about that before you busted my brother's head open, GET DOWN OR DIE, NOW JESSE." "She'll hate you for the rest of her life, did you think about that? You kill her brothers, any of us, she'll hate you. Can you live with that?"

Colt steps back, stunned at what he heard, knowing Jesse was right, she would. He was so angry he hadn't thought about that, could he do this, could he do this, to her? Could he live his life knowing she hated him? He thinks for a moment, and then looks at them: "Have no doubt, any of you, if you ever lay a hand on any of my family, ever again, I'll ride back from Hell if I have to, and kill every one of you, you got that?" "Yes, Colt, we do."

As he walks away, he hears them ride towards 'The Tall H' as fast as their horses will carry them. Colt sits on Rufus at the split in the road. He looks down one way, knowing she's there. He thinks about her in that orange dress and the softness of that first kiss. He is fully aware he didn't say it back. He turns Rufus to the west and rides.

Chapter Two:

A LONG WAY FROM HOME

Colt had ridden poor Rufus nearly into the ground. It has been months of aimless wandering, like a kite without a string. He went west toward California and north toward Montana, he didn't have a destination, he just knew he was a long way from home, and a long way from her. He rides upon a sign that says, Red Rock 2 Miles, he hadn't had a good meal, a bath and a soft bed in a month and he was ready for all three. Besides, who would have heard what he had done in a small place like Red Rock? He rides into town, it's a little bigger than he had anticipated, but still small enough where he felt safe. He rides up to the livery stable and slides off a tired Rufus, an old man limps out the open door:

"My daddy always said if we carried our horse on our back every once in a while, we'd show more appreciation for them carrying us." Colt understands the implication, and smiles in agreement, "Give him the best you got, he needs it. Where can I get a room and a meal?" The old man points down the street, "Mary Kelly serves a good meal, the only rooms are above the saloon, the beds are as hard as the whisky."

Colt walks down the street and sees The Blue Deuce Saloon, he decides a drink and a room would be first, he walks in, and to his surprise it's fairly crowded. He goes to the bar and orders a beer, as he begins to drink, he sees a man with a suitcase, a whisky drummer, who has the attention of everyone in the bar:

"That's right friends, I was right there, Colt McCoy came walking in the Golden Lady, his eyes focused on Two Jacks, you killed my friend, says McCoy, and I'm going to kill you, and your next," he said to Big Bob. Colt is horrified, he doesn't want to be recognized, but this guy is full of it, that wasn't how it happened, but he can't say anything so he turns his back to the drummer, not wanting the drummer to see his face.

"I tell you, friends, McCoy was as cool as a December morning. Two Jacks stood and said, I've killed men faster than you. McCoy said, you haven't seen anyone faster than me. He drew faster than anyone I've ever seen and shot Two Jacks right in the mouth. Big Bob went for his gun and McCoy shot his eye out. There is none faster, you can't be faster, I tell you. McCoy walked over to where Two Jacks was laying and said, that was for my friend Danny Boy, and walked out. I tell you friends, it was amazing."

Colt stands at the bar not knowing exactly what to do, this guy's not telling the truth, but was he there? Colt doesn't remember a whisky drummer that night but he really was focused on Two Jacks. "I hear he's on the run now," a voice from the back says.

"That's right," says the drummer, "I was there when the Marshall ran him out of town. He had just shot down Frank Davis, emptied his .45 into Davis without blinking. Davis didn't even have a chance to remove his coat, you know he always wore a three-piece suit. McCoy didn't give him a chance, he's fast, boys, like none you've ever seen. He stood over Davis, I think he wanted to take Davis's pearl handled pistols, when suddenly here came the Marshall and three deputies, all with double-barreled shotguns. Get out of town and never come back said the Marshall. McCoy looked him right in the eye and said, I'll leave, but it'll take more than you to stop me from coming back."

Colt looks at the whisky drummer and the drummer looks at Colt, he doesn't react, so he doesn't know who Colt is. "He can't be that fast," Colt hears someone say, "I promise you, he's not as fast as me." "Well, if you can find him, you can prove it," says the drummer. "I know how to find him, alright, I know how to make him come right to me." Colt looks over his shoulder and sees a thin man with a narrow face and mustache sitting alone at a table by the door.

"I'm the fastest gun alive, Whisky Drummer, and you'll be telling everyone you meet, how you met Johnny Duck, the man who killed this, Colt McCoy." The whisky drummer walks over to Johnny Duck, a little annoyed his story telling was interrupted, "So, how are you going to make Colt McCoy come to you, Mister Duck?" Everyone laughs.

"All I got to do is ride down to Deepwater and wait for his Pappy, or one of his brothers to come to town, if I kill one of them, he'll come running home, and there I'll be. Oh, I'll make it fair, or at least look fair, but he'll come running home, I promise you."

"Are you that fast Mr. Duck?" Again, there's snickers around the room, suddenly Johnny Duck stands, draws and fires, hitting a bottle sitting on the bar, "Is that fast enough, Mr. Whisky Drummer with a big mouth?" The drummer heads quickly back down the bar, "Oh, yes, that's fast, yes sir."

Colt can't believe what he just heard, this guy is going to kill his father or one of his brothers? What should he do? Maybe this guy is full of it too, but what if he's serious? What if he does nothing and this guy kills his dad, or Mark, or Ethan? He has, no choice, Colt turns around and faces Johnny Duck:

"You don't have to go through all that, I found you already Mr. Duck, with a Big Mouth." "It's him," the Whisky Drummer says, "It's Colt McCoy." Johnny Duck's jaw drops wide open, he stands slowly: "You McCoy?" "Yeah, I'm Colt McCoy, I heard what you said, so come on Mr. Big Mouth, you wanna be the fastest, then be the fastest.... ."

Johnny Duck goes for his gun, but he's not the fastest, he's not even close, Colt draws his . 38 and fires two quick shots before Johnny can clear leather, blowing him backwards and onto the floor. The place is deathly quiet.

Colt takes a deep breath and just shakes his head, then heads for the door, but he stops as he opens the swinging doors and looks back at the whisky drummer, "If you're going to tell it, tell the truth. My friend's name was Bud Miles." "I will son ... . good luck."

Neither Colt or Rufus got the rest they needed as they tried to put Red Rock as far behind them as possible. Colt was so tired he was about to fall out of the saddle and poor Rufus was tired, dirty and had a loose front shoe. They both had went about as far as they could go. Colt found a clearing beside a slow- moving stream, he slid off Rufus and took the saddle and bridle off and let him graze. Colt stripped down, and jumped into the water, it wasn't a hot bath but it felt good. Colt looked down stream, Rufus must have liked the idea too, he had waded in and was getting a cool drink. I'm going stay right here and rest for a couple of days he thought, and he did.

Colt is in the oak grove with Kay, she's wearing that orange dress, she's even more beautiful than he remembered and her kisses are sweeter than ever. He pulls her close and holds her soft body tight, he's going to tell her, he wants her to know, "Kay, I ...." Colt is awakened by the baying of cattle coming to the stream to drink, he raises up and sees two riders approaching: "Hey, Mr. Cooper doesn't take to saddle bums trespassing on his property." They get off their horses and start kicking Colt's things around, "Get your things and ride." Colt stands and faces the cowboys, "I'll leave, but you boys need to leave my things alone." "Did you hear that, Roy? He wants us to leave his things alone, I didn't know saddle bums had things," they both laugh. "I'm not a saddle bum, and I didn't know this was private property, but I'm not going to tell you again, leave me alone."

"I'd listen to him if I were you, you boys get back with the cattle." Colt turns to see a thin man, of about seventy, with graying hair sitting on horseback, "I'm Hank Cooper, the boys were right, you are on my property." "Ok, I'll leave," says Colt. "But I'm not a saddle bum and don't like to be treated like one." "I could tell, I kind of get the feeling it was a good thing I was here or I might have lost a couple of good hands."

Colt starts to pick up his things, "I don't know about that but I didn't appreciate the welcome." "What's your name, where you heading?" asks Mr. Cooper. "My name's Colt, and I guess I'm heading to wherever I can find a blacksmith, my horse has a loose shoe. Give me a minute and I'll leave ...." Colt had pretty much packed up his things and was saddling up Rufus.

"Maybe we got off on the wrong foot, the boys were just doing what they thought I wanted, we do get a lot of drifters going by this way toward Stillwater." Colt at least knew where he was now, Oklahoma territory, "How far to Stillwater?" he asked. "Too far to ride a horse with a loose shoe, I got a smith on the ranch, follow me and we'll get that shoe tightened up. There may be some leftover biscuits and bacon around somewhere, you never know."

Colt followed Mr. Cooper and soon arrives at a very nice ranch, the 'Bar C'. He stops at the barn where a blacksmith is working and Mr. Cooper instructs the blacksmith to attend to Rufus. He tells Colt to follow him up to the house and leads him to the kitchen. Colt sits, and isn't shy about accepting some of the leftover biscuits and bacon.

"You ever worked on a ranch Colt?" "Sure," answers Colt in between bites of what tasted like the best biscuit he ever had, "My dad has a small spread down in Texas, my brothers and I do our share." "I could use some extra help right now, if you're not in too big a hurry to get to wherever you're going, how about a job for a month or two?"

Colt thought for a moment, he could use the money, and if he stayed on the ranch, no one would know who he was, "Sure, Mr. Cooper, I'd like that." "That's great, just call me Coop, like everybody else, when you're finished, we'll go over to the bunkhouse and find you a spot."

Colt worked hard and it didn't take long to impress Hank Cooper or his fellow ranch hands. They could see Colt wasn't lazy and knew what he was doing. He stayed on the ranch and resisted the invitation of the guys to go to town on the weekends.

Colt had been riding fence all day, and was coming in late, when he saw the boys getting ready to leave for town. It was Friday and they usually quit a little early, put on their Sunday best, and headed for Stillwater. Colt went into the bunkhouse to clean up and then would see what the cook had saved him for dinner. He walked over and sat on his bunk for a second when Roy asked: "Who's your friend there, Colt?"

Colt looked down and there was a rattlesnake sticking out from under his bunk, his heart about stopped as he jumped up and staggered backwards, it was only then that he could see the snake's head had been smashed. The entire bunkhouse was roaring with laughter at the new guy. Even Colt got a laugh out of it when his heart slowed down.

Roy was laughing so hard, he could hardly speak, "Rudy almost stepped right on that thing earlier down by the barn, we see quite a few of them this time of year." Soon all the guys were heading out the door, Colt refused the guy's invitation to go to town and went to bed early, maybe he would dream again tonight, but he didn't.

The next day Colt was coming in from an early morning ride, he needed to cover one last area of fence he missed yesterday. He sees Roy and Mr. Cooper talking by the water trough so he got off Rufus and walked over to them. Roy was sitting on his horse and Mr. Cooper was standing close by.

"They shot all three of them, there wasn't anything I could do," Roy was explaining. "I know Roy, just stay clear of there, we don't need any trouble with them, we need to…" Mr. Cooper was saying when Roy interrupted: "Dang it Coop, don't move, there's one of those rattlers right behind you….." There, coiled up ready to strike, was a large rattler with its head and its tail sticking straight up in the air, the snake rattled and began to strike, Colt drew his . 38 and shot the snakes head off with one clean shot, twirled his gun once, and it was back in his holster.

Mr. Cooper never looked at the snake, it was Colt he was looking at, he had a look of total shock on his face. Colt kind of looked down with embarrassment, then glanced up at Roy who looked more amazed than Coop. It all happened so fast, really fast, that's why they were amazed. "You go ahead Roy," says Mr. Cooper, now looking down at the snake. "Sure Coop," Roy says still looking at Colt.

"That was pretty impressive Colt, thank you, you're pretty fast with that thing. You know, Colt, I never ask too many questions, what a man has done, and where he's been, is his own business." "I'm not a wanted man, if that's what you're thinking," Mr. Cooper. "I know most of the time when a man's fast with a gun, people think he's used it for no good, I haven't. I haven't broken the law and I'm not wanted. I respect you too much to do that to you. I wouldn't want to bring the law down here and do anything to harm you, or your reputation, I wouldn't do that."

"That's all I need to know Colt, that's good enough for me. But I've come to think a lot of you, and if you need my help, I'm here." "Thank you, sir," Colt turns and walks to the bunkhouse, after this, he could use a drink, he cleans up, jumps on Rufus and heads to Stillwater.

The town's full, it's Saturday night, there's a couple of saloons but he sees the horses with the Bar C brand on them tied in front of THE DRY GULCH, so he ties up Rufus and walks in. He sees the boys have a table over in the corner, so he gets through the crowd and surprises them. They sit and drink for a while, the boys still laughing about the snake under his bunk. He's grateful that Roy doesn't mention the other snake and his quick draw. He catches Roy looking at him a couple of times throughout the night, Roy knows something's up, he just doesn't know what.

Suddenly there's a commotion at the other end of the bar, "That's right, Johnny Dawkins took four to the chest and never got off one shot." You've got to be kidding me, Colt is thinking, not again. "Johnny Dawkins was a fast gun, but he was no match for Colt McCoy, and I'm gonna be that fast, I've been practicing and you can ask Darrell Woods how fast I am now." Colt asks Roy, "Who is that?" he can't see him through the crowd.

"That's Wild Bill, or something like that, that's what he wants to be called. His name is Billy Marcum, a stupid kid who wants to be a fast gun. About a month ago Darrell Woods, a local gun, was in here, drunk as a skunk. Billy was bragging about seeing McCoy kill Dawkins that night too, Darrell said he was tired of hearing about Colt McCoy, he and Billy got into it, the boy got lucky, shot him dead. Darrell was so drunk he could hardly stand up, never mind get his gun out of his holster, Billy was able to pull that old Army Colt he wears first. Now he wants to be another Colt McCoy, if he doesn't shut up, someone's gonna kill the man that killed Darrell Woods, if you know what I mean?"

"I know, exactly, what you mean," answers Colt. Colt leans back a little, trying to see through the crowd, finally, he sees this Wild Bill, Colt leans forward again, I know this guy from somewhere, but where? He takes another look and gets a clearer view, he sees the young boy, no bibbed coveralls or straw hat now, but he has that big old pistol wrapped around his waist, it's the young boy Colt was talking to when Johnny Dawkins came in the Golden Lady. That's right, he thinks, the kid said he had come down from Stillwater.

"Here we go," Colt hears Rudy say, "It's Orran, Roy, he's here." Roy explains to Colt, "That's Orran Wells, he's just a punk, but he was a friend of Darrell Woods, the farmer boy may be in trouble." The crowd starts to move to give them room, Colt can't see but he can hear, "You the farmer who killed Darrell? If he wasn't drunk, you'd be dead farmer boy. I heard you been in here running your mouth about wanting to be a fast gun. You want to be like Colt McCoy? Why don't you shut that big mouth and show us how fast you are…. ."

Colt jumps up and tries to get through the crowd, but it's useless, "NO, STOP," no one listens, then……two shots…… Colt pushes through the crowd, it's too late, Billy is laying on the saloon floor dead. Colt walks slowly toward the door, why would this young boy, anyone, want to live a life like this? Dear God, let it end. Colt rides back to the ranch alone, he lays in his bunk and thinks how much he needs to dream……. but he doesn't.

Mr. Cooper has Colt and some of the boys go up to the high meadow to move some cows, it's the first time Colt has been on this part of the ranch. There is about a hundred head of cattle there and the boys are slowly moving them along when Colt rides up to Rudy and Roy, who are stopped and talking.

"It sure is nice up here, why is Coop moving these cows, why not leave them here, there's plenty of grass?" asks Colt. Roy kind of hesitates and looks at the ground, "Well there's a problem with the water up here." "What, is it bad?" asks Colt.

"No, it's not bad, but the Mathew's claim the water, and there's been a little problem. I had a few of our cows up there last week and the Mathews bunch rode in, guns drawn, and shot all three of them, there wasn't anything I could do. They said for us to stay away from the pond, or else." "Is it on their property?"

"No, the pond is actually on both properties, but Jake Mathews claims it, and says he's going to fence it in. That makes this meadow useless because there's no water. Coop doesn't want any trouble so were moving the cattle down to a lower pasture Coop usually saves for later in the year." "I see." Roy kind of glances at Rudy then asks, "Colt, the other night in Stillwater, why were you trying to stop that gunfight?"

"I met that young farmer a while back, seemed like a nice kid, didn't want to see him get killed, what a waste." Colt doesn't say any more. Roy watches Colt ride away, he's figured it out. A few minutes later Rudy shouts to Roy," WHAT'S HE DOING?" Roy looks and sees Colt moving three cows quickly up the meadow towards the pond, Roy knows exactly what he's doing.

Colt is laying with his back to a big oak tree beside the pond. The cows have drunk their fill and are grazing with Rufus on the sweet grass near-by. In a pile on the other side of the pond is the wire fence and posts that had been around the pond. Colt hears riders approaching:

Colt stands and faces the five riders as they approach the pond. "What's going on here, who took down my fence?" asks the big man in the lead. "I did, my cows were thirsty," answers Colt. "Who told you, you could take it down?" the big man asks. "Who told you, you could put it up?" "I'm Jake Mathews, I own this pond."

"No sir," answers Colt, "You own half of it." The five riders spread out side by side, that's ok, Colt prefers it that way. "You can see there's five of us, right?" Colt nods his head yes, "I see that." "Are you telling me you're willing to draw against five men?" "Yes sir." Colt doesn't take his eyes off Jake Mathews. "Who are you, what's your name?" "My name's Colt, Colt McCoy."

For the first time since all this trouble started Colt wanted someone to know who he was, he wanted them to have heard of Two Jacks, Big Bob, Little Johnny Dawkins, Frank Davis or even Johnny Duck. The rider on the far right speaks up, "Colt McCoy? You wish you were Colt McCoy." "No, no I wish I wasn't, but I am."

Jake Mathews looks long and hard at Colt, "Does Coop know who you are? Did he hire himself a gun?" "No, Mr. Cooper has never asked me my last name, he has no idea, but you know, I want you to know, and to understand what can happen here." "Do you understand you could die here?" Mathews asks. "Sure, Mr. Mathews, but do you understand you could die here?"

One of the riders leans forward, "Jake? I think he 'is' Colt McCoy, he killed Frank Davis. Is a little bit of water, worth us all dying?" "You really think we're all gonna die, Earl?" "Yes, I do, Jake." "Would you really draw against five men?" asks Mathews.

"I've had men come to my home to kill me, rode hundreds of miles to kill me, die, wanting to make history with me. I saw a young boy lay dead, wanting to be like me, what are you going to show me here today I haven't already seen, death? I've seen that." "Yeah, I'll draw on you, I'll kill every one of you Mr. Mathews, but for what, some water?"

Mathews looks around for a second, thinking, "No, no,

I believe you would, it's not worth that. Tell Coop he can have all the water he wants." "You, tell him Mr. Mathews, you tell him when you pay him for the three cows you killed." Mathews looks at Colt and smiles, "You got guts boy, I'll tell you that. Ok, I'll tell him, let's go boys," they turn and ride.

By the time Colt got back to the bunkhouse to gather his things, the boys were gathered out front. Roy obviously had told them what he had figured out. No one said a word as Colt went in, gathered his things and came outside. "Be seeing you boys," was all Colt said as he got up on Rufus to leave.

It was Roy who stepped forward, "Colt, me and the boys have been talking, and we don't want you to leave. We all have heard what you've been through. It seems, to us, you had no choice in what you did. We all agree, we'll help you stand up to anyone who comes looking for you."

"Thank you, thank all of you, but this is why I left home to start with, I don't want anyone getting hurt on my account. Believe me boys, they'll come, from Fort Worth to Dodge City, when they hear that I'm here, they'll come. Thank you, but I better leave."

Colt sees Hank Cooper coming down from the house, "You know you can stay here, the boys and I talked about it." "Yes sir, and I thank you." "Well, if you're going to go, here's what you've got coming," he hands Colt an envelope that Colt can tell has a lot more in it than what he's got coming. "You've always got a home here if you need one Colt." "Thank you, Mr. Cooper," he turns Rufus, and rides.

Chapter Three:

A Shot in the Dark

Another long ride, another month in the saddle, Colt was tired and Rufus was getting contrary. They both needed some rest and Rufus needed some water. Colt rode over a hill and there was an old farmhouse, weather beaten and run down, there was a water trough out front and a few chickens running loose, so someone lived there. He and Rufus rode down hoping whoever lived there wouldn't mind if they had some water.

"Hello, anybody home?" Colt shouted as his sore body slid out of the saddle. "Put your hands up mister," Colt heard a voice come from the barn behind him. Colt raises his hands and looks toward the barn to see a boy about 10 years old with a rifle carved out of wood. "Don't shoot, Rufus here just needs a drink." The boy comes running and runs right up to Rufus. "Rufus, that's a good name for a horse," he takes the reins and leads Rufus to the trough. Colt hears the front door to the house open,

"Danny, what are you doing? Sorry mister, that boy loves animals," a frail old man, with gray hair, and a beard, walking a little hunched over, comes out onto the porch. "That's alright," answers Colt, "Sorry to bother you, we both just needed some water." "Help yourself, I'm Lee, just call me Pops, that's what everybody calls me, and I guess you've met Danny?"

"I'm Colt, and Danny's new friend is Rufus." "We're about to have breakfast," says Danny, "Can they stay Pops?" "Sure, it ain't much, but we'd like for you to stay." Colt joined them for breakfast which consisted of a piece of bacon, one egg and half of Danny's, day old, biscuit. Colt looked around at their humble home and wondered where Danny's parents were, he assumed Pops was Danny's grandfather. It looked like they were struggling, especially considering breakfast.

"We had rabbit last night for dinner, Pops used the last of the flour for gravy, it was good, wasn't it Pops?" Pops smiles, a little embarrassed, "It sure was Danny." Danny jumps up and runs out the door, "He'll aggravate that horse of yours, loves animals, that boy." Colt hesitates for a second, wondering how to ask, "Uh, Pops, where are we, exactly?"

"About four miles that way," he points, "You'll be in Kansas, but we're Sooners, you're in Oklahoma. You running from something, or someone, Colt?" "No, sir, I'm not a wanted man if that's what you're asking. I'm running, but just from myself."

"From the looks of Rufus, you both could use a rest. You're welcome to stay on here as long as you like. We don't have a lot, but we'd enjoy your company. Danny might end up sleeping with Rufus in the barn though," they both laugh. "Pops, I don't want to pry, but Danny's parents?"

"Danny's father was my son Carl, he and his wife Heather were in the bank over in Franklin six years ago, making the last payment on this place. Todd Mooney and his boys came in to rob the bank, the Marshall and his deputies tried to stop it. The shootout lasted about an hour before Mooney escaped, but when the smoke cleared, twelve people were dead, including my son Carl and Danny's mother. This place was a lot different then, we were trying to have something, but now, well, you see it."

"I'm, I'm sorry…. . you know, we are pretty tired, if it's not too much trouble, we may stay a day or two, is there a town close by?" "Sure, Liberty is about three miles west of here. A nice town, real nice people. I need to go to the general store anyways, Mr. Gravely may extend me a little, I help do some chores at the store sometimes, but it's been a while." "That's ok, Pops, I can find it. Maybe I'll get a few things while I'm there."

Colt rides into Liberty, it's a fairly small town, but a nice one. Has everything people need, general store, saloon, blacksmith, church, a real nice place where no one has heard of Colt McCoy, he hopes. He walks into Gravely's General Store, looks around, and then he sees her, wearing an apron covering a light blue dress, and helping a customer, she's the prettiest girl he's seen in a long time. He tries not to stare but it's hard not to, she has dark black hair, and the prettiest blue eyes he's ever seen. He acts like he's looking around but his eyes keep going back to her. He glances away for a moment and then hears, "Can I help you?"

To his surprise, it's her, "Yes, my name's Colt, oh, I mean yes, sorry, yes please," they both laugh at his awkwardness. "Ok, Colt, I'm Dianna, now that we know each other, how can I help you?" "Yes, I need some supplies, he starts to order, but orders more than he and Rufus can carry." "I'm sorry," he explains, "we just need so much."

"That's alright, I can have it delivered to you, where are you staying?" she asks. "I'm staying with Lee…. ." he realizes he don't know Lee's last name. Luckily, Dianna knows who he's talking about, "Lee and Danny? That's great, I haven't seen them in quite a while, I may bring this out myself." "Can I ask you something Dianna?" "Sure."

"Does Pops have an account here?" "Yes, I'm sure he does." "When I pay for these supplies, I want to pay whatever he owes." "That's fine but, I must tell you, it may be a little bit, he hasn't done well lately and.... ." "That's ok, it doesn't matter, one more thing, who could I see about buying some livestock?" She walks to the front door of the store, "You see that tall gentleman across the street talking to those men? That's Dale Ingram, he has what you need."

Colt pays for the supplies and talks to Mr. Ingram before heading back to the farm. As Colt approaches, he sees two men in front of the house, and it looks like Pops sitting on the ground. What the heck, what's going on? He then sees one of the men kick at Pops, knocking him over. Danny runs up to one of them and tries to kick him but the man grabs Danny and throws him to the ground. What in the world? Colt comes riding in at a full gallop and jumps off Rufus. "What's going on here?" he asks. Colt hasn't felt like this in a long time, not since Bud Miles. "We're just having a little fun," says one. "Since when is dying fun?" asks Colt.

One of them takes a glance at the other, "That look right there, is going to get you both killed, because I can promise you, the two of you aren't enough." Colt's trying not to lose it in front of Danny. "Unless you're tired of breathing, you better leave, because I promise you, I want to kill you right now, and I will, if you ever come around here again."

They gather their horses and start to leave, one of them looks back at Colt, "We'll be seein ya." "That's the Turley boys, from over the hill there, they're always coming around shooting my chickens and causing trouble," says Pops, getting to his feet.

Colt goes to his saddlebags and gets a bag of candy and gives it to Danny, "Oh boy, can Rufus have a piece?" They all laugh as Colt watches the Turley's ride over the hill. Colt doesn't say anything to Pops or Danny about his dealings with Mr. Ingram, he's busy repairing the chicken house and the coop. He's working on the fence when he sees a wagon approaching, he smiles when he sees who's driving it, it's Dianna.

"Wow, the place is looking better," she says as she exits the wagon. "They both will be surprised when Mr. Ingram gets here in a little while," Colt begins to unload the wagon. He and Dianna talk for a while, he was careful with his answers, but she was careful with her questions too. Colt helps her back up on the wagon, she smiles, and then heads back towards town. Pops and Danny come out of the house just as Mr. Ingram's wagons turn onto the property. "What's that?" asks Pops

"That's twenty-five, road island red, chickens and a sow with a big boar to mate her with. My daddy always said if you have a good sow, you may not get rich, but you won't starve." Pops hustles by to meet the wagons, Colt can see he's excited. Pops looks back at Colt, "You sure had a smart daddy, come on Danny."

The next few weeks were spent working on the farm and getting ready for their first litter of pigs, Mr. Ingram said this sow would be ready soon. The chickens were laying so many eggs, Pops was able to sell some. Colt was glad things were better here, Lee seems like a good guy, and Colt didn't want Danny to do without. Colt was sitting at the breakfast table with Pops when Danny came rushing in.

"They're here, they're here, ten of them, ten piglets, one of them is a runt, can I call him Petey, Colt?" "Sure Danny," says Colt being pulled by his hand out the door to the pen to see, Pops is right behind. Colt was repairing the pig pen when he saw a buckboard coming, he could see right away it was Dianna. He sat on the top rail of the pig pen fence as she exited the buggy and walked over:

"I brought some vegetables that were going bad, I thought your new arrivals could use them." "Thank you," Colt says, still sitting on the fence, "They do tend to make a pig of themselves," they both laugh and then, CRACK, the rail broke that Colt was sitting on causing him to flip backward into the pen, landing face first in the mud. Dianna has to hold on to the pen to steady herself she's laughing so hard. Colt looks up from the mud and is looking the big sow right in the face, he could swear that darned pig was smiling.

"Oh, you think this is funny?" he tries to get up, but that's easier said than done as he slips and falls back into the mud. Dianna is laughing hysterically. "How about a hug Dianna?" "Oh, Colt, you wouldn't?" she says running towards the buggy with Colt now not far behind. She runs around the other side of the buggy to get away from him, still laughing. He stops, a feeling of guilt comes over him, he realizes he hadn't thought of Kay in a couple of days.

"What's wrong Colt?" "Nothing," he says, looking at Dianna's beautiful smile. "I thought it was because you stink so bad. If you're coming to my house for dinner, you better take a bath."

Her house for dinner? "I'll take a bath, but for your parent's sake, not yours." Colt stood and watched Dianna ride away, he felt guilty about that too. He told himself not to, he told himself he probably would never go home again, never see Kay again, it didn't help. There was a chill in the air, he thought it might rain.

Colt rode through town to Dianna's house, when he arrived, there she was, on the front porch waiting, he stopped for a second to look at her, she looked beautiful standing there at the top of the stairs, he felt guilty about that too.

The dinner was good and he enjoyed talking to her family. Every now and then he would glance across the table and she would be smiling. It had been a long time since he had sat down to this kind of a meal, he had missed this. He visited for a while and it was getting late, Dianna walked him out to the porch.

"You're going to get wet," she said, there was a roll of thunder in the distance. "That's ok, I think I still have some mud behind my ears," Dianna laughs. Colt steps down one step, she draws close, he knows if he looks at her, he's going to kiss her, that feeling of guilt comes over him again. He walks on down the steps, creating some distance, then looks at her.

"Thank you, this is the best evening I've had in a long time." "You're welcome, Colt, maybe we'll do it again sometime." A light rain starts to fall, "I guess I better go, maybe I can beat the worst of it, goodnight." "Goodnight, Colt."

As he rode, he wished he had looked at her sooner. Colt rode through town and then out the west road toward the farm. The rain picked up a little and Colt heard a long roll of thunder, closer now. He rode a little faster, there was a flash of lightning......

Suddenly there was a CRACK.... a shot in the dark, a bullet goes through Colt's thigh, through the saddle and into Rufus. Rufus let's out an ungodly sound, there's another CRACK and Colt feels a burn deep in his back, another, and a bullet buries deep in the back of his left shoulder, another, but it was a miss. Colt can't breathe, Rufus is going around in circles making a loud cry, Colt loses the reins and is falling backward, he can't breathe, he twists and falls face first to the ground.

He hears Rufus, and then only the falling rain. The pain is excruciating, he struggles to get a breath, he closes his eyes... . he sees her sitting in church in that orange dress, he had burned that into his memory, he sees her sitting in the sun at the oak grove, he fights to breath, then............

Colt can feel something soft against his cheek and then he hears a soft voice whisper in his ear, "Don't die, please don't die, you have to fight, Colt." He feels her gentle kiss on his cheek, she's here, he turns his head to find her lips and her kiss is so warm and tender. This isn't a dream he thinks, she's really here. He tries to raise his arms to hold her but his left arm won't move, he reaches out with his right hand and she's there, he pulls her closer, this isn't a dream. He opens his eyes slowly and she 'is' here, but not Kay, it's Dianna. She slightly pulls away, he looks into those beautiful blue eyes, "Don't stop," he whispers.

Suddenly a sharp pain shoots throughout his body from his shoulder and back. He lets out a loud groan, the pain is almost more than he can bare: "Dear God, dear God, they've shot me all to hell." Pops comes to the bedside, "Don't you die, you hear me? I've lost one son, and I don't want to feel like I've lost another one."

He feels her head lay on his chest, "Pops? Pops? Rufus?" "Danny promised me that if I don't let you die, he won't let Rufus die. Dr. Thomas said the bullet went through your leg, and the saddle, which slowed it down, he was able to get it out ok. He won't be ready for a ride any time soon, but he's alive. He's in better shape than you are, get some rest, we're not going anywhere."

Colt barely opens his eyes, it's light now, he looks to the left of the bed and Dianna's asleep in a chair, Danny's standing right beside the bed, "Who's Kay?" he asks. "She's a friend of mine," Colt whispers. "You must like her, you talked about her a lot." "Yes, I do." It's hard to breathe, the pain….Colt closes his eyes.

"Colt, Colt, take this," he opens his eyes, it's dark again, Dianna has a spoon at his lips, "You need to take this broth, you need your strength." He shakes his head no and is out again. Colt wakes to the feel of a gentle hand brushing against his face, he reaches out for her, "Oh, Kay, it hurts so bad." What did he say? He opens his eyes and Dianna has a tear running down her face.

"Oh God, Dianna, I'm sorry." "That's alright Colt, I know I'm competing with a memory, that's hard to do, memories are soft, warm, and perfect. I can't be that, real life isn't like that." Colt has a different pain now, he's hurt her, he raises his right leg, bent at the knee, the pain is sharp, but he wants this pain, not the other, he can deal with this pain. He tries to sit up and almost screams with pain, he wants this, not the pain of hurting her.

"Stop it Colt, your leg is bleeding again, please." This pain is better, he doesn't want to feel the other. He tries to sit up again, the pain shoots from his back and shoulder, he about passes out. Pops comes to the bedside, "Please Colt, Doc said if you started bleeding again, he wouldn't be able to stop it, please."

He falls back, his head buried in the pillow, "Dianna, I know it's you, I know it's you……" She hugs him and he forces both arms around her, "It's ok, Colt, I know." She kisses his cheek gently and he holds her so tight, though it hurts, he won't let go. "Dear God Dianna, they've shot me all to hell." "I know Colt, just rest, I'm here, just rest." Colt mostly sleeps for the next couple of days. He tries not to move, the pain is unbearable. He's awakened by loud noises.

Colt wakes to the sound of gun shots 8, 10, 15, some pistol, some rifle, Danny runs in the door, "Stop them Colt, they're killing them, all of them, even Petey. They hurt Pops too, you said if they came back, you would kill them, do something Colt." There's the sound of laughter and voices. Danny buries his face in the bed, Colt reaches out through the pain and puts his arm around Danny, that's all he can do, for now. He closes his eyes, the pain.

Colt is awake but doesn't open his eyes to the darkness. He wonders if she's here, he needs her here, Dianna, her touch, her breath on his face, the touch of her lips on his, please be here. He opens his eyes to a nearly dark room. He can see Lee sitting at the table with a small candle burning. Danny is probably in his room but there is no one else.

"Lee? Lee? Pops?" he can barely say it. Pops raises his head, his eye is blackened where someone hit him, "We'll get it back Lee, I promise you, we'll get it all back. You tell Danny, I promise, we'll have it all again." Colt's breathing is short and fast. Pops comes over and stands beside the bed, "I know we will, I believe you…… I sent her home, Colt, it's too dangerous for her here right now."

Colt looks up at Pops, who smiles, Colt raises his right hand and Pops takes it, "You just rest, let them think that you're dead, we'll have our day. You and I both know it will take more than these two back shooters to kill……Colt McCoy." Colt smiles and nods his head, so Pops knows, he closes his eyes, and rests.

Colt sits on the side of the bed, he was able to eat, and his breathing is better. He stands and about falls back onto the bed but steadies himself. His recovery has been long and slow. He looks around the room, looking for something, Pops asks, "Is this what you're looking for?" he holds up Colt's gun. "Yes," he puts the holster on, "Hey Pops, is there any hickory trees around here?"

The night is dark and rain is falling, Colt rides slowly down the street of Liberty. He hopes to find what he's looking for at the saloon. They think he's dead, but he's far from it now. There's a score to settle with the Turley's, not just for what they did to him, but what they did to Lee, and Danny. This may mean he'll have to move on, that's ok, he knew how life would be when he left Deepwater. But this is ending here, tonight, no looking back wondering or worrying, this ends now.

Colt stops at the saloon, ties Rufus to a hitching post and removes his poncho. He walks in the swinging doors and looks around, and sure enough, sitting at a table with two other cowboys playing cards, are the Turley brothers. Colt walks slowly towards their table, one of the Turley's looks up, a look of total horror comes to his face, like he's seen a ghost. His brother then looks up and his eyes widen:

"I'm Colt McCoy, and I'm going to kill both of you." "One of their friends says, "Colt McCoy?" and stands like he may want to challenge Colt. Colt looks at him, "I'm not here for you, don't die over this." Their friend looks at Colt and can see the look in his eyes, he changes his mind and both of their friend's head for the back door, leaving the Turley's alone.

Colt looks to the Turleys, "I'm gonna have them bury you ten feet deep." "Ten feet?" asks one of the Turleys. "That's right, I want you as close to Hell as you can get." One of the Turley's does a very bad imitation of the Missouri Quick Draw, Colt draws and fires one shot to his forehead, he staggers backwards and slides down the wall.

"Please don't kill me, we didn't know it was you," says the other. "To shoot somebody in the back, does it matter who they are? Then, to do that to an old man, it's an old man and a boy, what did they ever do to you?" Turley, raises his hands, he slowly lowers his left hand to release his gun belt. "You wouldn't shoot an unarmed man, would you?"

"Don't do it," Colt says walking quickly towards Turley, kicking a chair out of the way, "Don't do it, or so help me, I'll kill you anyway, draw you coward, draw or I'll kill you where you stand." Turley lets out a scream of absolute fear, "Ahhhhh," he goes for his gun, Colt draws and shoots once, Turley staggers back, Colt fires again, Turley's back is to the wall, Colt fires again, Turley falls to the floor.

Colt takes the money off the table where the Turley's were seated, "You owe them this," Colt says, looking down at the Turley brothers lying on the floor, he turns and leaves. The sun is starting to rise as Colt puts his packed saddlebags on Rufus and ties them down. The door opens and Lee comes out, he walks slowly up to Colt, "Where will you go?" "I don't know, anywhere, it doesn't matter."

"Colt, I don't know how to thank you, not just for what you tried to do here, but for being more than a friend to me and Danny. It felt good to have someone here again, to laugh again. I wish you didn't have to go, but I understand. I want you to know, "I love you son, and we'll never forget...." he wipes a tear from his eyes.

"No, Lee, I thank you, for giving me a place to be normal for a while, to feel like I had a home again. Tell Danny good-bye for me, and Lee, Mr. Ingram will be making a delivery here today, that should make Danny happy. I promised you that we would have it all again, I may not be here, but I'll always feel like I'm a part of this place." "You always will be, son."

Colt gets up on Rufus, he has a stop to make before leaving. Colt rides through town and sees there's still some activity at the saloon, he rides by, no one notices. As he approaches Dianna's house, he sees her sitting on the top step, like she's waiting. Maybe she knew he couldn't stay, he wouldn't stay, word travels faster than lightning, and trouble will come. She sees him and stands, he slides off Rufus and enters the gate, he starts to run, no words, up the steps and into her arms. There are no words to explain how he feels right now, and he won't let himself feel guilty about that.

"I'm sorry Dianna, that I didn't tell you who I am." "That's alright Colt, it wouldn't have mattered." "I don't know how to thank you, I'd be dead if not for you, you gave me reason to live, reason to breathe. Holding you in my arms, those intimate moments with you, made it worth all the pain, I'll never forget...."

"I know Colt, I won't forget either........ especially you in that pig pen," she smiles through her tears. She hugs him tight, she can barely speak, "Please be safe, please, will it ever end Colt?" "I guess it will eventually, somehow, in some saloon or another rainy night, but I don't know if I would change a thing, Dianna. I think every one of them got what they deserved, and the day is coming when I guess I'll get what I deserve too." He doesn't want to leave, but it's time, he looks at her one last time, turns and walks away. Colorado maybe, Nebraska? He and Rufus ride on.

Chapter Four:

WICHITA

Why would anyone trade a good life, being able to go where you want, do what you want, to live like this, to be known as a fast gun? Maybe they think it's a glamorous life, but they've got a surprise coming, it's been a very lonely way to go for Colt, and he don't know how much more he can take. He's been up through Colorado and Nebraska and isn't sure, exactly, where he is now. He has avoided most of the big towns and a lot of the small ones, he wants to go home, to see his mom, dad, his brothers, and even if it's for the last time, he wants to see Kay.

He hopes she's happy, it's been so long, she has probably forgotten, and he couldn't blame her, yes, it's been a long, lonely ride. Colt hears a train whistle and comes over a hill to see a train pulling a long line of cattle cars. There's a big herd of cattle grazing and he can see a town in the distance. He's low on money and patience, he doesn't care, he's going to town.

He rides past the grazing herd and soon sees a sign that says: WELCOME TO WICHITA, so he's in Kansas, he hopes the town is too busy to notice one lone rider. Sure enough, the town is busting at the seams, the cattle pens down by the railroad are full, there's several herds waiting outside of town to be loaded, the town is full of cowboys and money. Colt finds a place to eat, and as darkness falls, he goes into the closest saloon.

It's packed with cowboys fresh off a cattle drive, who want to drink and spend their money. There's plenty of card games and dance hall girls, Colt finds it easy to blend in, he stands at the bar drinking a beer. He's either going to have to find a job or try his hand at poker. He's a decent poker player, but with limited funds, he will have to find a small stakes game. Suddenly he's bumped into by one of the girls who's having trouble with a drunk cowboy:

"Come on Maggie, one little kiss, just one won't hurt nobody." "Now Sam, I can't do that, go buy one of the other girls a drink and be a good boy." The cowboy reaches out to grab her, "Come on Maggie…." Colt reaches out and grabs him by his wrist, "Now, my Maw and Paw wouldn't like you trying to kiss my sister in public like this."

The cowboy looks at Colt with a puzzled look on his face, "This your sister?" "Sure is," says Colt. "I'm sorry sir," he tips his hat to Maggie and staggers off into the crowd." "Thank you, cowboy, it's good to have a kid brother around when you need one," they both laugh. Maggie is an older woman, probably been doing this a long time, she's wearing a lot of makeup and is, very exposed, in her working clothes.

"These cowboys buy you a few drinks and they think they have something coming, my name is Maggie," she says. "Glad I could help, ma'am, I'm Colt," Colt watches her as she grabs another cowboy's arm that walks by and goes back to work, "Have a good night, Colt." Colt looks around, surveying the room, there's three cowboys, one with a big white hat, and there's a rather plump gentleman wearing a tight suit smoking a cigar playing poker over in the corner. Colt walks over to the table, seems like a small enough game.

"Room enough for one more," asks Colt. "Just a friendly game," answers the cigar smoking player, "Have a seat, ten-dollar limit." The dealer with the big white hat just looks up but doesn't look, really happy. Colt finds a seat between the two cowboys who look at Colt but don't speak. The deal goes around the table, after a few hands Colt's breaking even.

White Hat has the deal again, and as slick as you please, Colt sees him give Cigar a couple of cards from the bottom of the deck. What the heck's going on here? These two guys trying to steal money off two cowboys in a small stakes game? That doesn't seem like it's worth risking getting in trouble, and these guys may be in trouble.

Colt gives White Hat a long cold stare, he wants him to know he saw him, White Hat sees Colt looking and the hand continues, Colt drops out, and Cigar, sure enough, wins the hand. The next few hands are fine and White Hat is dealing again, this time he deals Colt a couple of cards off the bottom. Colt wonders, now what's going on? He looks at his hand two aces and two eights, commonly known as a dead man's hand, maybe White Hat is trying to tell him something. There's a pretty nice pot and Colt wins. Colt wants away from this crazy game but it will look bad, quitting right after winning a big hand.

Suddenly Colt feels an arm around his neck, it's Maggie, "I wondered where you went, you promised to buy me a drink, come on, Cowboy, you can play cards later." White Hat speaks up, "Looks like you got a different game to play, it's not nice to keep a lady waiting."

Maggie drags Colt, willingly, away from the table. They go to the bar, "Thanks," says Colt, "I wanted out of that crazy game." "Oh. Honey, you were in the wrong game, they're reeling in a fish and you dove into the pond." "Yeah, I like my cards delt from the top, and he's not very good at it."

"You don't have to be good if nobody's looking, you give

the fish a couple of good cards and while he's looking at his great hand, you deal your friend a better hand. They've been doing this all week." "So, I guess, White Hat and Cigar are together?" asks Colt.

"Oh, no, Cigar is the fish, the other three are together. They're letting him win a few hands, they've only taken him for about a hundred, just enough where he wants his money back. Watch this, the two cowboys will start to argue, they will bet against each other but Cigar will think he's got the winning hand, watch." White Hat deals giving Cigar a couple of cards from the bottom, while he looks at his hand, one of the cowboys gets three quick ones.

"You've been trying to bluff me all night, my grandmother can do better than that," says one cowboy to the other. "I'll show you a bluff," he looks at White Hat and Cigar, "I know we have a ten-dollar limit but I want to shut this big mouth up, can we drop the limit for this hand?"

White Hat throws his cards in, "I'm out, you do what you want, how about you? he asks Cigar. "I'll pay, just to watch, go ahead," says Cigar. "Here's a hundred, now that's no bluff," says one cowboy to the other. "Well, I think you are bluffing, here's your hundred and I raise you two," the fish is being reeled in.

Cigar throws three hundred into the pot and watches. "Here's your two hundred and two hundred more, still think I'm bluffing? Put up or shut up." "I'll call that bluff," the cowboy throws two hundred into the pot. "Well, boys, let me get into this game," says Cigar, throwing four hundred into the pot," I raise two hundred myself." The cowboys call his bet.

Cigar lays his hand on the table," Sorry boys, but I've got four pretty ladies," he lays out four queens. The first cowboy throws his cards into the pile," beats me mister." Cigar starts to rake in the large pot when the other cowboy speaks up as he lays his cards down," Not quite partner, I've got four gentlemen, four kings, looks like I win."

Cigar is shocked, he looks around the table, he knows something's wrong here, he just got taken, but he doesn't know exactly how. White hat is looking at him with his hand under the table, and there's probably something in that hand. Cigar quickly gets up and leaves the saloon.

"See what I mean?" says Maggie, "He let you win one, but he may have been sending you a message. It was best you got out of the way." "Here, take this for your help," Colt gives her a twenty, "I appreciate it." "Thank you," she says, hiding the twenty, where women hide things when they don't have pockets, "You might have found yourself in trouble, little brother." "Not as much trouble as them," Colt tips his hat, Maggie looks at him quizzically as she walks away.

The two cowboys leave the table and go their separate ways, White Hat collects the money and walks by Colt as he leaves, "You did alright, didn't you?" he asks Colt as he walks by not looking at him. "Yes, but I prefer my cards from the top." "Me too," says White Hat walking out the door.

Colt decides to stay in town a couple of days, it's so crowded with so many cowboys coming into town, he can stay unnoticed. He is up early and is walking down the sidewalk, he's going to try to get some breakfast before the town gets busy. He's lost in his thoughts as he walks, he's thinking of her all the time now, he wants to hold her, feel her lips on his. If he closes his eyes, he can almost feel her. He has to get back to her somehow, this nightmare he's lost in, has to end, but how? His thoughts are interrupted by a young boy standing in front of the general store.

"HERE IT IS, RIGHT OFF THE PRESS, GET YOUR COPY, 'THE MAKING OF A FAST GUN, THE STORY OF COLT McCOY.' GET IT FOR ONLY A DIME." Several people stop to buy a copy of what is referred to as a dime store novel. Colt can't believe it, it's been nice being in town, around people, he hopes this doesn't change things. Colt walks by the young boy, his curiosity gets the best of him, and he gives the kid a dime and buys one of the books. He's curious to see how accurate it is. He reads it over breakfast and is surprised to find it is very close to the truth. The whisky drummer actually told a factual account of what happened with Johnny Duck. There's so much more to the story, so much people will never know.

Colt is back in the saloon and the place is packed again. There's plenty of cowboys wanting to have fun and spend their, hard earned, money. Colt looks around the room as he's having a beer, and there is White Hat and his two friends, at it again, this time with an old cowboy as their fish. Colt is watching them when Maggie comes to the bar to get someone a bottle from the bartender:

"Give me a bottle Sam," she sees Colt, "Well hello, little brother." "Maggie, how are you this evening?" asks Colt. "I'm ok, little brother, how are you?" "I see they're at it again," referring to White Hat and his friends. Maggie looks over in the corner, "Oh no, that's Jed, he'll be ruined."

"Who's, Jed?" asks Colt. "There's not a girl in here Jed Lane hasn't helped at one time or another. He's the sweetest old man you'll ever meet. I know he sold his cattle yesterday, but he needs that money to get through the year, he'll be ruined."

"Who is this White Hat and his friends? Are they from around here?" "Well Honey, he calls himself Doc, but he's no doctor, I shouldn't say this, but, that's Todd Mooney and his boys. Tried his hand at about everything crooked at one time or another, including bank robbery, and now he's running this crooked card game, poor Jed, I wish I could help him."

Todd Mooney? Colt knows that name, Pops said it was Mooney who was holding up the bank the day Danny's mom and dad were killed. "Maybe I can help Maggie." Colt starts to walk towards the card game. Maggie grabs his arm," Who 'are' you, you don't scare easy do you?" "Well Maggie? I'm your, long lost brother, and no, I don't."

Colt goes over and sets his beer on the table, "Another friendly game boys, mind if I set in?" Colt doesn't wait for an answer he sits down beside Jed. Todd Mooney, is obviously annoyed, he shoots Colt a dirty look. Mooney is about to deal as Colt reaches for his beer with his left hand. "Hey Todd, I mean Doc, me and Jed would like to have our cards off the top of the deck, if you don't mind."

"What do you mean by that?" Mooney stares at Colt. "Well, it's just your fingers get confused sometimes when you deal," he looks at Jed, "You know what I mean Jed?" Jed has a confused look on his face, he stands and picks up his money off the table, "I think I need a drink," he walks to the bar.

Mooney is fuming at Colt, "I'm amazed you're still alive the way you poke your nose in someone else's business." "I'm amazed your still alive, Todd, killing innocent people robbing a bank and dealing, very badly, from the bottom of the deck." Both of the cowboys are on the edge of their seats, "What's your name so we'll know what to put on your tombstone?" asks one of the cowboys.

"Right now, I'm the man who has a . 38 pointed under the table at your boss, the rest of the time they call me Colt McCoy." The two cowboys sit back in their chairs, whether it's his name or the . 38, they're not going to make a move.

"Two of the people killed in that Franklin Bank were the parents of a friend of mine, Todd, or should I say, Doc? It may not be here, unless you and your friends want to die here, but we will meet again, and I won't be unarmed like those people in the bank."

"I see, Mr. McCoy," says Mooney, collecting his money and standing to leave, "I look forward to that meeting, I hope it's soon," he and his partners leave. Before he can stand, Jed Lane and Maggie come over and sit down," I owe you son, I would have lost my farm if it wasn't for you, and I thank you," says Jed.

"That's alright sir, glad to help." Maggie looks at Colt, "Who are you, where are you from? I don't see men like you come in here very often, if ever." Colt looks down, "I'm nobody special, just passing through." "I think you're special, real special," Maggie smiles. "If you don't mind me saying so, I think you're special too," Jed raises his drink as to drink a toast to Colt.

Colt gets up early the next morning, he walks down the sidewalk thinking it may be a good day to leave. The weather is nice and he's just about stayed as long as he dares in Wichita. His thoughts are interrupted by a commotion in the ally by the saloon. A crowd gathers and he watches from across the street, he sees Jed Lane come through the crowd. Jed doesn't see him but is walking straight to him,

"Good morning, Jed, what's going on over there?" "Oh, Colt, it's Maggie, they beat her bad." "What?" Colt takes off running and pushes through the crowd. The doctor is there but doesn't seem to be doing much and when Colt looks at Maggie, he sees there's not much to be done, she's been brutally beaten. Colt kneels down.

"Hey, Maggie, don't move, just be still." "Hey, little brother," she whispers, she's barely breathing, "I told them I didn't say anything, I didn't tell who he was, he wouldn't believe me." "I'm sorry Maggie, I got you into trouble, I'm so sorry." She looks at Colt, "Who are you?"

"I'm Colt McCoy, Maggie, and I promise you they will pay for this, I'm so sorry." "Colt McCoy? I told you, you were somebody special……. ." Maggie's dead. Colt's not in such a hurry to leave anymore.

Night falls, and Colt stands in the shadows in the street, this feels familiar to him, he's done this before. He starts to think, about all he's done, he's not as innocent as he would like to think. He's taken it upon himself to right the wrongs of this world, and that's not his right to decide. He's stayed, just on this side of the law, and even that doesn't give him the right to do anything. He told Dianna he would get what he had coming someday, maybe he'll get it tonight, who knows? But he waits, right or wrong, for Mooney and his friends. The wheels of justice turn slowly, but Colt is anything but slow.

He waited for a long time and just when he thought these men probably cleared out of town, he sees the two cowboys, without Mooney, ride up to the saloon and tie up their horses. Colt steps out of the shadows: "What kind of coward does it take to beat a woman to death?" asks Colt.

The one cowboy steps out into the street, "I'm not afraid of you McCoy." "I really don't care whether you're afraid or not." "I never did think Frank Davis was that fast, anyway, and Maggie wasn't nothing but an old wh........." Colt draws and shoots him in the throat, the cowboy grabs his throat and blood is pouring through his fingers, Colt walks toward him," SHE WAS A WHAT? COME ON, SAY IT, YOU'RE NOT AFRAID, SAY IT NOW, WHAT WAS SHE?" the cowboy's gagging trying to breathe, he falls to his knees and then face down in the dirt.

Colt turns to the other cowboy, "Please Colt, please, I didn't do it, it was Mooney, I swear, let me get on my horse and I'll be home in Missouri by morning, I'll ride all night, please." Colt realizes what he just did on the streets of Wichita, is he this kind of killer, has he become an animal? People are watching in horror, at what he just did, "Get away from me now before I change my mind," says Colt. The cowboy is quickly on his horse and ridding out of town.

A crowd is gathering, Colt doesn't care if they know

who he is or not anymore. Jed Lane steps out of the crowd and comes over to Colt: "You alright?" Jed asks. "Yeah, I'm ok, I'm sorry about Maggie, it was my fault."

"You can't take responsibility for the actions of a madman, Colt. No way, you nor I, could have seen that coming. Maggie told me she knew this Mooney from back in Kansas City, I think they were more than friends back then. She hadn't even told me who he was until after that card game. But she didn't deserve to be beaten like that, he'll get what he's got coming."

"Yeah, I guess we all will," Colt starts to walk away. "WHAT'S GOING ON HERE?" it's the Marshall of Wichita. Colt hears Jed talking to the Marshall, giving him a chance to keep on walking, "There's one of the men that killed Maggie, he just picked a fight with a young man and got killed in a fair fight, I saw it all Marshall." "Thanks Jed," says the Marshall, "You boys help me get him off the street and over to the undertaker."

Colt, walks down the street, he could use a drink but doesn't want to go into a saloon. Maybe someone heard, and knows who he is, he doesn't want more trouble tonight, there's so many cowboys in Wichita right now. He sees a Mexican Cantina and goes in, maybe it will be safe in here, he gets a beer and sits alone at a table. He gets a few glances, most of the cowboys prefer the saloons, he's the only 'gringo' in the place, he likes it this way.

He drinks his beer and thinks of her, her eyes, her touch, her kiss, he must find a way back to her, but there is no way. His reputation is growing, dime store novels are being written about him, killing the murderer of a saloon girl in Wichita will only add to the story. There must be a way, there has to be a way:

"It must be a lonely life, to be hunted by so many, my friend?" Colt looks up and doesn't recognize the older Mexican gentleman, it sounds like he knows who Colt is. "My two sons, were killed in a place called Allura, by an evil man called Dawkins. My sons were hired to put up a fence, they did not know there would be trouble, they did not carry a gun. This man, Dawkins, shot them down like dogs and left them to die. When I heard this man was shot down by an honorable man, whose only wrong, was that he stood up for his friend against two evil men, I rejoiced that good had overcame evil."

Colt's not sure what to say. "Do not be distressed, my friend, if evil follows you, evil will always follow good, as the darkness will always follow the light. You have been called to bring justice to those who cannot stand for themselves. There have always been men like you, this world has always needed men like you, my friend. To be the voice of them that cannot speak, to be the light that chases the darkness. Do not be distressed, you have brought honor to those who have been wronged, evil must never have the last say."

The old gentleman turns and says something in a loud voice to all in the cantina, Colt doesn't speak Spanish, so he has no idea what he said. Everyone in the cantina yells with a loud voice and stands, raising their drinks into the air. "They will not drink, until you raise your glass and drink, my friend, Mr. Colt McCoy." Colt stands and raises his drink, "Thank you, my friends," Colt drinks, and the place explodes with laughter and music, for a while he can forget, and know he's among friends, and he does, way into the night.

Colt wakes to the sound of a train whistle, they are constantly coming and going, he lays in bed for a while, thinking of her, he can't stop, he sees her face and her smile, he must think of a way back to her, but the events that have unfolded have left no escape. He leaves a constant trail for those to follow who want to kill him, and only no good can come from being around those he loves.

He'll leave today, he's seen enough of Wichita, and

Wichita has seen enough of him. Colt packs and is preparing to leave when there is a knock at the door: Colt opens the door to the Marshall of Wichita, who has a copy of the dime store novel about Colt in his hand," Good morning, Mr. McCoy, I'm Dan Wash, the Marshall of Wichita." "Good morning, Marshall, I was just leaving."

"Well, that's what I was coming to talk to you about, Jed Lane explained what happened last night, and I'm satisfied, that it was a fair fight. But you and I know that there will be those who will follow you, wanting to enhance their reputation. Quite frankly, Mr. McCoy, I don't want to die trying to run these fast guns, who are wanting to kill you, out of Wichita. More importantly, I don't want any of my people here to die either."

"Like I said, I'm leaving." "I wanted to ask you, Mr. McCoy, about this book, how factual is it?" "Surprisingly, Marshall, it's pretty close." "I'm not saying you're totally innocent, no man is, but if this book is accurate, I'm sorry then, that things have turned out this way for you. I wish I had an answer as to how you can get out of this, but when you killed Two Jacks, that's all it took. To kill one notorious gunman, starts a wildfire you can't put out."

"Yes sir, I know, I'm packed up, I'll leave now Marshall." "Thank you," the Marshall leaves. Colt gets Rufus saddled and walks him out of the livery stable. He's just about to put his foot in the stirrup when he hears: "Colt McCoy, you're a hard man to find, I've been looking for you." Colt turns, he knows this boy from somewhere, but where, "Who are you?" Colt asks.

"I'm Oran Wells, I guess a man should know who it is that's going to kill him." Oran Wells? It's the kid who killed Billy Marcum back in Stillwater, "Go home Oran, leave me alone." "I've came a long way to kill you McCoy and I'm not leaving until it's done, now draw!" Colt draws, fast as lightning, Oran is standing there with his mouth open, gun still in his holster,

Colt doesn't fire but stands there looking at him:

"Here, you want to be known as a fast gun, you want to be known as the man who killed Colt McCoy?" Colt throws his gun on the ground, "Shoot me, go ahead, you think you're fast, there's a hundred men that will come after you, and I guarantee you, at least one of them will be faster than you. One Oran, that's all it takes, kill me, do me a favor, this life isn't nothing like you think it is, you want it? Be the man, or leave me alone."

"I'm, I'm sorry, Colt, you could have killed me dead, I've never seen anything like that, I don't want that kind of life, you can have it, I'm sorry," Oran turns and walks away slowly. Colt picks up his gun, climbs up on Rufus, and rides.

Chapter Five:

THE HANGING

Colt had ridden east, into Missouri, he found a good place to camp by a river and just wanted to rest for a few days. He had caught a couple of fish and was just getting ready to put them on the fire when a voice caught him by surprise: "Hey, you in the camp, mind if I come in?" "Ok, I guess," answered Colt.

A young boy, about eighteen, rides a tired old pinto into the camp, "Thanks Mister, been on the move for the last few days, you're the first person I've seen." Colt looks at the boy, he looks like he's been on the move alright, dirty and probably hungry, "I was just getting ready to put a couple of fish on the fire, you're welcome to one of them, if you're hungry?"

"If you've got a line and a pole, I'll catch my own." Colt points him to his pole and the boy heads over to the river. To Colt's surprise, the boy catches two nice fish pretty quick, cleans them and comes back to the camp. "Always did like fishing, back on our farm, there's a nice fishing hole not far down river, we had fish more than we did beef. If you would do me a favor, Mister, and put these fish on the fire for me, I've got something I need to do."

"Sure," says Colt, wondering what it was he needed to do. The boy walked down to the river, took off his boots, and leaped right in, clothes and all. After a few minutes he got out, stripped down, as far as he dared, came back to camp, and hung his clothes over a low hanging branch. "Sorry mister, but that was for your benefit as well as mine. I was getting pretty rank."

Colt smiles, "I guess I should thank you for washing up for dinner." "Nice to meet you, I'm Colt." "Nice to meet you Colt, I'm Luke Parker" The boys ate fish and sat around the fire, talking about hunting and fishing, but the obvious questions were coming, "So, where you from Colt?" "A little town in Texas, and you?" "Me? I'm from right here in Missouri, not too far from here, but lately, I've been moving around pretty quick."

"Is there a reason for moving 'quick' Luke?" "I'm not a wanted man, so don't be afraid the law's gonna raid your camp or anything, but I do have those who will be looking for me now." "If you don't mind me asking, why would someone be looking for you, did you do something to somebody?"

"I killed a famous gunfighter, and you know how it is, there will be plenty of men wanting to face me down, to make a name for themselves," Luke has a stick he's burning the end of it in the fire. "Oh, really?" asks Colt, wondering who this boy might have killed, looks like they may have something in common.

Colt didn't want to ask so he just let the boy talk: "Yeah, I was in a little town called Uwell, up north of here, when he rode in, I didn't know who he was at first. I'm not a fast gun, so I don't know much about such things, but I guess it was fate. We were in the saloon and there's a girl who works there named Maria, who's sweet on me. This guy was buying her drinks and he started making unwanted advances toward her and when he wouldn't stop, I called him out. He went for his gun, and I went for mine, I guess I was faster and there he lay on the saloon floor."

"And he was famous enough to where you think you had to go on the move?" asks Colt. "Oh, he was famous alright, they don't come any more famous than the man who killed Frank Davis, I killed Colt McCoy, there will be plenty of men looking for me." "Colt McCoy? You killed Colt McCoy?" "Yeah, hard to believe, isn't it? But I tell you, I did."

"Yeah, that is, hard to believe, how do you know he was this McCoy fella?" Colt asks, really intrigued at what the answer will be. "It was him alright, no doubt, with his .38 Colt Navy Revolver and riding a big roan. He was fast I tell you, but he missed, I heard the bullet whiz right by my ear, he was famous for his head shots you know. But I didn't miss, thank goodness, now I'm a man on the run."

"Oh, yes, I see." This boy is obviously lying, but this is a dangerous game he's playing, if he keeps telling this story, someone will believe it and will want to kill the man that killed Colt McCoy. Colt's not sure what to do about it yet, so he leans back and just watches the fire and soon goes to sleep, the young boy does the same.

Colt dreams that he sees her, neither one of them says a word, he is just staring at her, she's coming closer, she's beautiful, he can see every detail of her face, he's about to kiss her when Colt is awakened by the rustling of Luke putting fish on the fire, "They sure were biting this morning," Luke says, putting four nice fish on for breakfast. Threw four or five back and just kept the biggest ones, you better wash up, these will be ready soon."

Colt lays there for a minute trying to remember as much as he could about his dream. He finally gets up and washes, and they sit down to eat, Colt don't know what to do about this lie that Luke is telling. How many other people has he told this to? He definitely doesn't want to be the reason some fast gun shoots this boy down, but what to do, tell him who he is? "So, where you heading Colt?" "I don't know, is there a town near here?"

"Hey, I never asked, are you a wanted man Colt? I can help, I know this place like the back of my hand. If you want to stay away from people, I know this place where no one will ever find you." "No, I'm not wanted Luke, but you need to know...." Luke interrupts, "There is a town near here, Dry Creek, they have a real mean Marshall, but if you want to go there, I'll go with you, I'm not afraid or anything. If you need supplies, they will have what you need."

"Dry Creek, I've never heard of it, but I do need a few things. I guess if we behave ourselves, the Marshall won't mind if we stop in. By the way, Luke?" "Yeah Colt?" Colt stops, "Never mind, let's get going," Colt figures there will be a better time to tell him.

The boys ride into Dry Creek, it's a nice town, not too big, like a lot of towns Colt has seen lately. They stop at the General Store and Colt buys a couple of things, Colt notices that Luke is getting some strange looks from some of the people, he hopes Luke hasn't spread his story around here, it could be dangerous for both of them.

Colt would like a drink but doesn't know what to do with his new found friend, "I was thinking about getting a drink but.... ." "Sure, that's a good idea, let's go," says Luke heading for the saloon. "Well, that's not what I meant........ but sure, why not?" Colt says, mostly to himself. Luke and Colt walk into the saloon, the bartender is sweeping up a broken mirror, Colt notices that Luke is still getting some funny looks. He really hopes no one in the saloon has heard this lie, that's all he needs, to have to defend Luke for this ridiculous story he's telling, and besides, Colt doesn't like the part where he said Colt was harassing some girl.

Colt gets a beer, and to his surprise, Luke orders a

whisky. Luke drinks it down in one swallow and starts to cough and hack, "Hey, slow down there, buddy," says Colt, "Have you ever...." Luke's already ordered another shot, and quickly swallows it down. Colt gets the feeling this may be Luke's first drink, that feeling is substantiated when Luke starts to wobble and his speech is slurred. One of the cowboys at the bar buys Luke another drink, why would he do that? Then another cowboy buys him another drink, and Colt wonders, what's going on here?

Then the last thing Colt needs, starts to happen, Luke starts to talk, "I can't stay here, boys, you know why I can't stay? I've got to move because I killed...." Colt grabs Luke and starts to drag him towards the door. "He can't stay because he killed about a half bottle of whisky and it's bed time," Colt just wants to get Big Mouth out of there before he says anything else. "We don't blame him for wanting a drink, with his brother going to be hanged and all," says one of the cowboys.

"What?" asks Colt, Luke is too drunk to comprehend. "His brother, they're going to hang him on Saturday for cattle rustling. They caught him red handed with two of Mack Stafford's cows, the law says they hang rustlers, they're going to do it at noon on Saturday." Colt drags Luke out the door and somehow gets him to the livery stable. He lets him pass out into a pile of hay and Colt goes to talk to this, mean Marshall, Luke was telling him about. Colt goes to the Sheriff's office and, the Marshall is there, he's an older man, and if he's mean, he sure doesn't look like it.

"Marshall, I understand you're having a hanging on Saturday?" "Unfortunately, yes, a local boy was caught rustling and the law is very clear on that, as much as I hate it, Saturday at noon we're going to hang him." "I happen to know his brother, Luke, I was hoping there was something I could do."

"If paying for the cows were an option, I'd do it myself. This boy's family is so poor, and there's about eight kids, the cows wondered on to their property and the boy butchered one of them to feed the family," the Marshall pours himself a cup of coffee. "What if Mr. Stafford dropped the charges?" Colt asks, hoping there may be a solution.

"That would be fine, but he isn't going to do that, this family has been like a thorn in his side for years, Mack Stafford owns all the land around their farm, he's always wanted to expand his ranch but the Parkers won't sell. And besides, he's lost enough cattle to rustlers over the years, he would have hanged him his self if I didn't stop him."

"I see," says Colt, "I was hoping I could do something." "I wish you could son, but there's nothing to be done." Colt looks at the Marshall, "Do you mind if I ask you something? The rumor I heard was that you were a pretty mean guy to recon with, but you, actually, seem like a pretty nice guy."

The Marshall laughs, "How did I get that kind of reputation? Well, I'll tell you how reputations get started: About three years ago a guy by the name of Vinny Dugan came into town. Vinny had a reputation as a pretty mean guy, he got drunk and started shooting up the saloon. My Deputy and I went down there, and it just so happened I took a double-barreled shotgun with me. The place had cleared out and Vinny was shooting and hollering, he shot through the window and nicked my deputy in the arm, I instinctively, shot both barrels of my shotgun through the window."

"The yelling stopped, and when we looked, Vinny was dead, he had been standing on the other side of the window. The next thing you know, I had the reputation as being someone you didn't want to break a law in my town, not a bad reputation to have as a lawman, but I'm not, that kind of a guy. I'll tell you this, If I can make it until my Deputy gets back from fishing next week, me and my reputation are going to retire, I've been doing this for thirty-five years, and I've had enough."

"Yes, I know all about reputations, good luck with your retirement." Colt leaves and goes to collect his new best friend. How in the world can he tell him about his brother, and what will Luke do? Colt takes Luke back to the river and lets him sleep it off. Colt is up early the next morning and has breakfast almost done before Luke starts to wake. He can only hope that Luke doesn't overreact to the news, the Marshall said the only solution was if Mr. Stafford dropped the charges, there has to be a way to make that happen.

Colt is starting to put some things together now, Luke being poor, one of eight kids, he may have left home to make it easier on his folks with one less mouth to feed. He probably made up this crazy story to cover up the fact that he's just a poor boy wandering around. Colt doesn't want to embarrass him about being poor or telling a lie, but he has to know about his brother.

Luke sits with his head hanging down, Colt has just told him and he's not taking it well, "Henry is the oldest and tries his best to take care of the rest of us. Don't know nothing but farming, but we hardly have money for seed. Mr. Stafford's cows wonder over on our property all the time, we had joked about butchering one of them, but I never dreamed he would do it. Things are pretty bad right now, we have six sisters, and you can only catch so many fish."

"I'm really sorry Luke, I wish there was something I could do." "There is something, Colt, you can help me break him out of jail." "Now wait a minute Luke, that's not a good idea, first of all, I've got my own problems and don't need to cross the law, and the last thing you need is to get yourself killed, and maybe Henry too, by doing something stupid." "That's the only answer Colt, I can't let my brother hang, I just can't do it. With or without you, I'm going to bust him out."

"Listen to me Luke, we've got three days, don't do anything crazy, give me a chance to figure something out. You don't want to be on the run the rest of your life, believe me, it's not a good life. We've got three days, the Marshall said if Mr. Stafford dropped the charges, Henry wouldn't hang. Let me talk to him, maybe we can work something out. Just promise me you won't do anything yet, ok?"

"Ok, Colt, but if we can't figure something out, I'm busting him out," Luke stands, "I need to go and talk to Henry and make sure he's alright." "Let's eat breakfast and we'll go talk to him and I'll see about having a talk with Mr. Stafford."

After breakfast, Colt and Luke ride back to Dry Creek, there's a large crowd gathered in the street. The boys tie up their horses and try to get through the crowd to see. Colt hopes it doesn't have anything to do with Henry, he hopes he didn't try to escape or anything. When the boys get through, they see the Marshall, standing in the street with a double-barreled shotgun. Also in the street are three men, dirty clothes and unshaven, facing off with the Sheriff:

"We told you, our brother ain't staying in no stinking jail for two months, you let Orvil out right now Marshall." "I told your brother to stop making trouble or the next time I'd lock him up for sixty days, he threw a bottle through the mirror in Dusty's Saloon and I locked him up. He's got fifty-nine days to go and I'm not letting him out till then, now you boys go home, you're just going to make things worse."

"We ain't going nowhere without Orvil," the three men spread out," You only got two shots in, that there shotgun, Marshall, how you gonna handle three men?" Colt steps down off the sidewalk into the street and faces the three men with the Marshall, "Not a good way to head off into retirement."

"You're right about that," says the Marshall. "So, who are you?" one of the three asks Colt. "I'll tell you who 'I' am," Luke says walking over beside Colt, "I'm the man who killed

Colt McCoy." There's a gasp heard from the crowd. "No, he's not," says Colt, "I'm Colt McCoy." There's another gasp heard from the crowd. The men and the Marshall look confused, "He just said he killed you," says one of the three.

"Well, he didn't." "Who *are* you?" whispers Luke to Colt. "Look, my names Colt, I have a .38 Colt revolver, ride a big roan, from Texas, you figure it out, I'm Colt McCoy." "Hey," says another of the three, "If you're Colt McCoy, how you alive if he killed you?"

Obviously these three aren't the three sharpest tools in the shed, but it is a legitimate question, "You ain't no ghost, did he kill you or not?" Luke whispers to Colt, "You're not Colt McCoy, you can't be, YES, I DID KILL COLT McCOY," Luke shouts to the three men who look totally confused now.

"NO, HE DIDN'T, I AM, COLT McCOY," shouts Colt. "Are you one of those aborigines?" asks one of the three. "It's not aborigines, you idiot," says his brother, "It's apollonian." Colt answers, "I think you mean apparition, no, I'm no ghost." "So, you ain't dead yet?" "No, not yet," says Colt.

The Marshall, and the crowd, looks confused too, "This is the darndest gun fight I've ever been involved in," the Marshall turns to the three men," LISTEN, THIS IS EITHER COLT McCOY, OR THE MAN WHO KILLED COLT McCOY, EITHER WAY, GO HOME, SO I CAN FIGURE IT OUT."

The three men look at each other, and walk away scratching their heads," We'll be back in fifty-nine days to get Orvil." Luke looks at Colt, "Are you really Colt McCoy?" "Yes, I am." "Why didn't you tell me?" "I didn't want to call you a liar." "Well, obviously, I am, a liar." The Marshall looks at them both, "Do you think we could go to my office and get off the street, everybody knows who you are now." "Oh, Colt, I'm so sorry," says Luke, "My lie, my big mouth, everybody does know who you are now, I'm so sorry."

"That's fine Luke, you have to admit, that was nearly the darndest gunfight you'll ever see," they all laugh and head to the Marshall's office. "Thank, you boys, for your help, things were about to get serious, good thing you came back from the dead to help, Colt." "I didn't even know I was dead, till I met Luke." "I guess you'll be on the move again, because of me," says Luke. "Not until I talk to Mr. Stafford, will you show me where he lives?" "Yeah, I will, I guess I better go home too, Ma and Pa are probably a mess over Henry."

The boys ride east of town towards the Stafford ranch and Luke's home. When they get there, Colt is surprised at the size of Luke's farm, it has potential, but you can tell they are poor. The farm is almost surrounded by the Stafford ranch, It's like it's right in the middle of a horseshoe. It's easy to see why Mr. Stafford would want to buy it, big fields and access to water. It may be the only way to get Mr. Stafford to drop the charges, to offer to sell it. Colt hopes not though, he knows how it would feel if his family had to sell their property after all the hard work that went into it.

Colt stops at Luke's place long enough to meet his family, and it is painfully obvious, they are very poor. The girls, all six of them, come running out, they are really glad to see Luke, and his parents are nice, but Colt could see their concern for Henry. Colt soon rides toward the Stafford's, he hopes something can be done, but he's not sure what.

Colt rides onto a very busy, and a very impressive ranch. A large two-story house, plenty of cattle and a large corn field, a very nice place. Colt knocks on the door and asks to speak to Mr. Stafford, he's invited in, and waits. A balding, overweight gentleman soon enters, "I'm Mack Stafford, how can I help you? If you need a job, I must tell you, I only hire experienced men, but I pay top pay for hard work."

"No sir, I don't need a job, I wanted to talk to you sir, about Henry Parker." "Well, you're wasting your time with that, he's going to hang Saturday, he stole two of my cows, and that's the law." "I know that's the law, but if you were to drop the charges, the hanging would be called off." "I can't do that, you see......."

The door opens and a young man hustles in, Colt can't help but notice a scar above his left eye, running down to his cheek bone, "Pa, you'll never guess who I heard was in town?.. .. Oh, I'm sorry to interrupt." "As I was saying, I can't drop those charges," continues Mr. Stafford, "I get enough cattle stolen as it is, if I don't show people what will happen, it will open the door for more rustlers to come in here and wipe me out."

"Pa, you'll never guess who's in town?" the young man says again. "Wait a minute son." "You know the Parkers don't have much, you can see how they live, do you really want to take away their oldest.... ." "Pa, he's in town, I just heard...." "Excuse me," Mr. Stafford says to Colt, "Who's in town son?" "Colt McCoy, he's in Dry Creek."

Colt's not sure where this is going, so he waits, he can't help but look at the boy's scar, it's terrible, and he's so young. "Let me take care of business here and we'll go see," Mr. Stafford says to his son. The boy notices Colt looking at his scar and looks down with embarrassment. "Sorry, I couldn't help you?. .... oh, excuse my manners, what was your name?" Mr. Stafford sees his son's reaction to Colt looking.

"This is my son, Andrew, I guess you noticed the scar, he was on a cattle drive, down in Texas, when he stopped to have a beer with the boys. There was a rather large man in the saloon they called Big Bob, Andrew here got a little tipsy and this Bob fellow started a fight, not a very fair one, he beat Andrew while his friend, Two Jacks Akers, held a gun on the boys to keep them from helping. He's a little excited, he heard the man who shot these two is in Dry Creek. We wanted to meet him, so if you'll excuse me Mr. ? .... I'm sorry, I never did get your name?"

"It's McCoy, Colt McCoy." Both of their jaws drop and their eyes grow wide, "Are you serious, you're Colt McCoy?" asks Andrew. "Yes, I am." "Is it true that you shot Big Bob's eye out, and you shot Two Jacks in the mouth?" "Yes, it's true, I didn't plan it that way, but they killed one of my best friends in an unusual way, and maybe somewhere deep in my mind, I wanted them to die, in an unusual way. I'm not proud of it, but I wouldn't change it now."

"You can see what they did to me," Andrew says, turning his head to give Colt a better look at his scar. "I'll tell you this Andrew, don't let that scar define who you are, let how you carry it, tell people who you are. A scar doesn't tell people what kind of a man you are, your actions do. They got, exactly, what they deserved, let it go, and move on."

"You're right Colt, I will." Mr. Stafford looks at Colt, "You go tell the Marshall to let that boy go, that's the least I can do for you. It must be hard to have to leave home, and I've read what you've had to do to stay alive, and we're glad you have." "Thank you, Mr. Stafford, can I suggest something to you?" "Sure," he says, putting his arm around Andrew's shoulders.

"I understand you would like to expand." "Yes, I would, but the land is limited around me." "I saw the huge cornfield, you have, wouldn't you like to run cattle on that land instead of corn?" "Sure, I would Colt, but I need the corn for feed, and we have a large garden on there too. It takes a lot to feed the animals and people on this ranch."

"Well, Mr. Stafford, there's the Parker farm, large fields going unplanted, why don't you let them raise your corn and winter wheat, as well as your garden, that's what they do, they're farmers. You could make a deal with them that would free your land for cattle, and they would thrive also, raising your crops."

Colt could see Mr. Stafford's mind working and he's smiling, "That's perfect, that would help us expand our herd and help them too." Mr. Stafford starts to give Andrew orders, "Andrew, take a couple of wagons into town, buy enough food to stock the Parkers kitchen, everything they need. Tell Mrs. Parker and the girls to come over here and get what they need out of the garden. Give Mr. Parker two hundred dollars in case he needs to hire more help. Buy enough winter wheat for them to plant, it's not too late for that. Mr. McCoy, you have no idea how good it has been meeting you."

"Thank you, so much, Mr. Stafford, I'll tell the Parkers they are now in business with you. They will be so happy, and happy about Henry too." Colt tells the Parkers the good news, their life will never be the same. Luke is preparing to go to town and get Henry," I'm sorry about my lie Colt, I guess you'll be leaving because of me?"

"I would have had to move on anyway Luke, I can't stay anywhere for long, I'm glad this worked out for your family and for Henry." "How can I ever thank you Colt? I can tell you I'll never forget you, and I won't forget that crazy gunfight we almost had either," the boys share a laugh. Colt climbs up on Rufus, and they're on the move again.

Chapter Six

A Face in the Crowd

Before now, Colt didn't care what direction he was going, east, west, north, south, it didn't really matter anymore. But this time, for the first time in a long time, he knows where he is, and where he's going, he's heading to Dodge. He knows it's full of gunmen, who would love to know who he is, and gain the reputation of gunning him down. Why then, why, go to a place like Dodge? It's not a death wish, at least he tells himself it isn't, Colt is tired, tired of running, tired of living like this, maybe it's time to put an end to this, whatever that means.

Darkness had fallen and Colt found a place in a grove of pine trees. He built a small fire and was laying back, thinking of her, he hadn't dreamed much lately, seems like dreams are all he's got to look forward to anymore. He stayed awake, thinking about all that's happened and all the people he's met. It wasn't all bad, he's tried his best to help people, he's done some good. But killing seven men doesn't have a very good sound to it, no matter who they were.

Dodge will be full of cowboys, with the cattle drives being this time of year, gamblers, fast guns, everyone will be there. He tries to convince himself this is the right thing to do. This isn't a death wish, it really isn't, so then, why go there? If Colt thought Wichita was booming, it's nothing compared to Dodge City, there's cattle by the thousands waiting to be shipped. The streets are crowded, and so are the saloons, day and night. Why is he here, what does he want, what does he want to happen here? Who knows at this point, he didn't even know.

Colt finds a place for Rufus, and a place to eat. He heads toward the nearest saloon which takes him past the General Store, he looks through the window, and there it is, a stack of the dime store novels, THE MAKING OF A FAST GUN, THE STORY OF COLT McCOY. It serves as a reminder, that this is going to follow him, no matter where he goes. He can't outrun it, and he can't outlive it.

Colt enters the Lonely Widow Saloon, it's packed, he finds a spot at the bar and gets a beer. After a while, he happens to see a familiar face, back in the corner playing cards, it's Todd Mooney. He doesn't recognize anyone else at the table but it's Mooney alright. Colt is too far away to see if Mooney is, reeling in a fish, but he figures he is. Colt was contemplating, whether to interrupt the game like he did with Jed Lane, when suddenly a cowboy jumps up from the table:

"That last card, came off the bottom," the cowboy says going for his gun, as he draws, the cowboy sitting to his right, grabs his arm preventing him from drawing his gun for a split second, Todd Mooney draws and shoots first, the cowboy falls dead to the floor. Mooney collects the money from the table, and he and his two partners, head out the front door.

Colt starts to follow them, but he waits, this may not be the opportune time to do this, he'll deal with Mooney sometime, not just yet. The cowboy is carried out, and things settle down, everyone gets back to drinking and playing cards. Colt has a few more beers, everything is pretty quiet now, Colt has just about had enough for the night when he hears someone say: "I've waited a long time for this, turn around."

He didn't want this, not now, he just got here, and it didn't take long to be recognized. Now someone was going to die, was it his turn? "I said turn around, I heard you said you were the fastest gun alive, let's see just how fast you are." Colt slowly puts his beer on the bar and begins to turn around when the man beside him turns around first and says: "I may not be, the fastest gun alive, I hear the McCoy boy may be that, but I'm faster than you."

Colt steps aside, they weren't talking to him, but they were talking about him. "I'm Newt Maynard, and I say I'm the fastest gun alive, and I'm the man who's gonna kill Terrance James." The two men draw and Terrance James, who had been standing beside Colt, draws first and shoots Maynard in the chest, Maynard falls to the floor, James shoots him twice more.

"So, you're Terrance James? I don't think your that fast," says another cowboy standing up from a near-by table. James shoots him twice, without saying a word, quickly reloads his gun, looks around, as if to see if there was anyone else wanting to try him, then walks out of the saloon. Three men dead his first night in town, this place is wide open. Maybe it was a mistake to come here, whatever he needs, whatever he wants, is not here. He needs her, he wants her, and she's not here. He'll leave in the morning, there's a better place to be than Dodge.

Colt could hardly sleep with the streets full of cowboys all night, he wants to put this town behind him as soon as possible. He goes down to the livery stable to get Rufus, and to his surprise, Rufus is gone. There's a lot of horses being boarded, some in the barn, some in the corral, but Rufus isn't anywhere to be found. Colt, starts to panic, his friend is gone. He finds the owner of the livery stable:

"Where's my horse?" "How am I supposed to know?" says the owner. "I left him with you, where is he?" "Buddy, I'm too busy to keep track of your horse every minute of the day." Colt draws his gun and places it to the side of the owner's head, "How busy are you now?"

"Alright, alright, a big roan, yeah, a girl rode him out of here about an hour ago, I couldn't stop her, she went by me so fast headed out of town that way," pointing west. "That horse is the best friend I've got, if I don't find him, I'm coming back here, and Colt McCoy, is going to kill you, you got that?" The owner's eyes are about to pop they're open so wide, "Yes sir, Mr. McCoy, dear God of all the horses to take."

Colt saddles up the owner's horse and rides west as fast as he can go. With all the cattle coming into town and all the cowboys, it's impossible to track Rufus, there's nothing distinctive about his tracks so they just blend in. Colt rides the road west and hopes he can catch them. He has to find him, Rufus may not only be his best friend, but he may be his only friend, they've been through so much together.

Rufus is big and steady, not built for speed, but he can go all day, after a couple of hours, Colt finally catches a glimpse of a horse in the distance. He's about ridden this horse into the ground so he hopes he can catch up soon. He catches another glimpse and it appears there's two people riding Rufus, he knows this old nag of the owner's is about to break down, soon Colt realizes he can't catch them, he's lost his friend.

The owner of the livery stable said it was a girl who stole Rufus, why would a girl steal a horse, and why was there two people ridding him? Colt sits in the shade letting this old horse the owner gave him rest. He knows Rufus is getting farther and farther away. After, an hour or so he decides to try it one more time, he doesn't want to give up on his friend. Colt mounts the owner's horse and heads west as fast as the old boy will go.

Luckily, Colt goes around a bend and sees two young girls swimming in the creek, Rufus is tied to a near-by tree. Colt slips up on them, not being noticed, and unties Rufus. He notices the girl's clothes hanging on a limb, so he takes them too. The girls continue to play in the water and still don't notice Colt sitting on the old horse, holding Rufus's reins, and their clothes.

"Howdy," says Colt, startling the girls who keep their selves hidden under the water, considering he has their clothes, which they haven't noticed he has yet. "Thought I'd come, and take my horse back, you know they hang horse thieves around here." "Is that really your horse?" asks the older of the two girls. "Sure is, the best friend I've got. If you hadn't stopped, I probably wouldn't have been able to catch you."

"So, what are you gonna do?" asks the younger of the two. "I guess I'm going back to Dodge, but how do you like being stolen from?" he says holding up their clothes. "What?" "What?" they're both hysterical, because they're both in their underwear. "I'll be seeing ya, well, you better hope not," he says riding away.

"WAIT, WAIT, MISTER, PLEASE," Colt can hear them as he rides. "MISTER PLEASE," he can still hear them panicking. Colt starts to laugh as he turns around to go back. They see him coming and hide in the water. He throws their clothes on a bush and turns away to let them come out and dress. "That wasn't very nice," says the oldest girl.

"It wasn't very nice of you to steal my friend." "It was an emergency." "Oh, really, what kind of emergency makes it right for you to steal my horse?" "Well, well," she hesitates, "None of your business." "It's also none of my business how you get to wherever you're going," Colt turns and heads back toward Dodge. After a while he looks back, and in the distance, he can see the two girls walking. He sits there for a second, and then rides back to the girls, "I guess you rode him out here, you can ride him back."

The girls eagerly jump on Rufus's back, after a few miles, the owner's horse totally gives out, they're going to have to camp for the night. Colt builds a fire and they get as comfortable as they can. They talk into the night and Colt finds that the girls are sisters, Jean is the oldest, fourteen, and Kassey is ten. They live on the outskirts of Dodge, and their mom works at The Lonely Widow Saloon.

"Where were you going with Rufus if you live in Dodge?" asked Colt. The girls were really reluctant, to answer, "You weren't running away, were you?" he asks. "Kind of," answers Kassey. "Kind of, how do you kind of run away?" "We had to go somewhere, before…."

"Before what Kassey?" She hangs her head, "Our Pa left a long time ago, Ma ain't married but Grady lives with us. ." "He's disgusting," adds Jean. "He won't leave us alone, if you know what I mean? We can't stay there any more, we'd rather run away." "Did you tell your mom?" "She stays so drunk, and she's never home, we hardly ever have food to eat, and look at our clothes, she doesn't care. We'd be better off running away."

Colt and the girls talk, then Colt lays back and stares into the fire thinking, he watches the girls sleep soundly knowing they're safe. He can't take them back, at least not back home. He falls asleep and has another dreamless night.

Colt and the girls ride back to Dodge, he has the girls wait as he goes into the livery stable to talk to the owner: "I see you got him back," the owner says nervously. "No thanks to you," answers Colt, "I'm going to leave here in the morning, when I get here, I better find my horse, or I'm going to set fire to this place with you in it, you understand me? You better sleep with my horse, if you have to, and make sure nothing happens to him."

"Yes sir, Mr. McCoy, I will sleep with him, if I have to, no problem, he can't snore as loud as my wife anyway," he laughs nervously, "Yes sir." Colt has a plan, so he moves quickly, he takes the girls to the general store and buys them each a new dress and new shoes. He feeds them a good breakfast and then they head to the train depot. Colt is talking to the ticket master when he hears: "WHERE YOU GIRLS BEEN? YOU WAIT TILL I GET YOU HOME." Colt turns to see a nasty looking man in dirty old clothes, with rotten teeth, holding the girls by the arm. "YOU KNOW WHAT I'M GONNA DO TO YOU WHEN I GET YOU HOME?" Colt draws his gun and places its barrel against the man's temple, "They're not going home with you."

"Who are you? These are my girls." "I'm Colt McCoy, you heard of me?" "Yes, I heard of you," he answers nervously, not moving an inch. "You let go of these girls before I blow what little brains you've got out of your head." He slowly let's go of the girl's arms. "Now you listen to me, if I ever see you again, I'm going to kill you. If I see you from a mile away, I'll shoot you from a mile away, you got that?"

"Yes, you'll never see me again, I swear." "Now you leave here, if you look back, I'll shoot you right between the eyes, do you believe me?" "Oh, yes, I believe you." "NOW GET......." He takes off running almost falling down, not looking back. "You girls alright?" Colt asks the girls, he can feel some people starring at him, they not only saw what he did, but they heard who he said he was, but he doesn't care right now, he has something to do.

"Take these," he hands them two train tickets. "You get on this train, you'll be on it all day, take this," he hands them a piece of paper. "I had the ticket master write down what you need to do to make it to Deepwater, Texas, where I live. If anyone says anything to you, you tell them you're Colt McCoy's sisters, they'll leave you alone. When you get to Deepwater, the Marshall will get you to my parent's ranch. My mom always wanted a girl, now she'll have two." The girls hug Colt tightly around the neck, "Thank you, thank you, so much."

"Take this so you can eat," he gives them some money, "It will be a long trip, but you'll be ok, you've got each other.

When you get there, you'll meet your two new brothers, tell them all I said..........." he thinks about how long it's been, it's been a long, long, time, he fights back the emotions, there's so much he'd like to say, but he can't, "Tell them I'm ok, and give them this for me," he hugs the girls tight as if he were hugging each of them back home. The girls get on the train, Colt waits till it leaves, waving at the girls looking out the window, they look so different now. Colt turns away, back to......?

The next morning Colt saddles up Rufus and rides past the train depot heading out of Dodge. He happens to look at the people who are getting off the train and he sees a face in the crowd. Is that who he thinks it is? He stops and tries to get a better look, and sure enough, it's Jesse Harris, standing on the platform holding a suitcase. Colt rides over and jumps off Rufus, he doesn't bother to tie him up, "JESSE, JESSE?"

"Colt, is that you? What in the world are you doing in Dodge?" "Trying to leave mostly, how are you, Jesse?" "I'm good Colt, the question is, how are you?" "I'm ok, I guess, staying alive." "I see that, it's good to see you, Um Colt, that thing with Ethan I'm......" "Oh, don't worry about that Jesse, that's long behind us now, how is my family?" "They're all good, is there somewhere good to eat around here, I'm starved? Let's sit, and I'll catch you up about everybody." Colt gets Rufus and he and Jesse go to sit down and talk over breakfast, there's a lot to catch up on.

"Well, Ethan finally married June last summer, and you're going to be an uncle soon. Your folks are fine, Mark is fine, the ranch is doing really well. I told your dad to sell his cattle up here like we did, the prices here are really high, but he sold to a drover from down home, did well though."

"How's your family Jesse?" "Everyone's fine, Pa has pretty much turned the ranch over to us boys, so we stay busier than ever." Colt waits, he knows it's coming, he didn't want to seem anxious: "Colt....... about Kay, well, Kay's getting married Colt. You know it's been two years.... ?" What? Two years? Colt's mind starts to race, has it been that long? Dear God, two years......

"For the longest time, she would keep looking at that oak grove hoping to see you there. I actually caught her there crying a month ago. Two years, not knowing if you're dead or alive, buried somewhere, or even married yourself, who knew?"

"I don't blame, her, two years is a long time. I wanted to come home, I couldn't, I just couldn't. I don't want her holding on, she needs to move on, she deserved better than this, living like this, like a hunted animal."

"I don't envy the life you've had to live Colt. I can't imagine what it's been like for you, and I hope I never have to find out. But she waited, and we just left her alone, we figured either you would come home, or time, would take care of things in the end. She and Mike started seeing each other a few months ago and they're getting married, well, actually soon after I get back, they're getting married in three weeks." Three weeks, Colt lowers his head. "I've got to cash this money draft at the bank, what do you say, let's tie one on in Dodge tonight?" asks Jesse. Colt smiles, "This place gets crazy after dark, let's us two Texas boys show them we can get crazy with the best of them."

Colt walks over to the bank with Jesse, Colt waits outside as Jesse takes care of his business. Jesse comes out of the bank and inadvertently bumps into a cowboy walking with two of his friends: "Watch where you're going boy," the cowboy says to Jesse. "Excuse me," Jesse says. "There's no excuse for you, I may have to teach this boy some manners, Kansas style. Where you from boy?" "Texas, and I said excuse me," says Jesse. "I never did like you Texas boys," the cowboy says getting face to face with Jesse. Colt takes his left hand and pushes Jesse back and he steps forward, "What's wrong with us Texas boys? Why don't you tell me?"

The cowboy steps back, as to size up Colt, "Wait a minute

Ray," one of his friends says, "You know who this is? This is Colt McCoy, I saw him about blow a man's brains out at the train depot." "Are you Colt McCoy?" the cowboy asks. "Do you really want to find out?" Colt replies. "No, No, I don't believe I do, let's go get a drink, boys," the cowboy tips his hat to Jesse, "Excuse me," the three of them hustle on down the street.

"So, is that how it is Colt?" asks Jesse. "Sometimes...sometimes not... let's get drunk, Texas style." The boys have a real good time, Colt thinks of her a few times throughout the night, but mostly it's two friends having fun. They meet for breakfast the next morning, both of them have Texas-size hangovers, Colt's saddled up and ready to leave, "How long you staying Jesse?"

"I have another deal to settle, a couple more days, I guess. I'm traveling with a couple of other ranch owners for safety. I'll wait for them to finish their deals. There will be quite a bit of money on the train home so it's good to travel together. But, I have to get back as soon as possible to get things ready for the wedd……. well, back to the ranch."

"It's been good seeing you Jesse, take care, tell everyone I said, hey." Colt climbs up on Rufus, "Hey, Colt?" says Jesse, "Take care of yourself, you hear?" "Sure will." "And Colt, about that thing with Ethan?" "It's all forgotten Jesse." "Thank you Colt, I mean that," Colt starts to ride away, "Stay alive Colt, whatever it takes.

Colt rides out of Dodge, it was good to see Jesse, but it feels good to put Dodge behind him. Colt rides for a good part of the day, passing the swimming hole where the girls were, the sky grows dark, a light rain starts to fall. Colt continues to ride, it's getting dark now, he hears the roll of thunder in the distance. It reminds him of the night he was shot and it all almost ended. Maybe he would have been better off if it had ended there that night? He's thought of her all day, he's thought of the wedding, twenty days now. Colt brings Rufus to a stop, he sits there in the rain. He turns Rufus to the south, and heads for Deepwater.

Chapter Seven:

DEAR GOD, LET IT END

Twenty days to go 700 miles, Colt rode Rufus all night. He finally stopped when Rufus starting acting like he had enough. Thirty-five miles a day only puts him there the day of the wedding, that won't be soon enough. Colt's mind is spinning a lot faster than 35 miles a day. He stops for the night and doesn't bother to build a fire.

He wakes, and is in the saddle before daylight, Rufus can go all day, but is it fair to ask him to do that, for ever how many days it takes to reach Deepwater? No, it's not, Colt don't want to ride Rufus into the ground, and that's exactly what will happen, if this continues. But for now, until he figures this out, this is day twenty.

All he wants to do right now is to get out of Kansas, and even that, isn't happening fast enough. It's 250 miles to Oklahoma and he's ridding like he's trying to get there today. He hadn't thought about food, stopping to eat is out of the question. He also seems to be following the storm that passed through yesterday, it's rained all day today. Rufus is a trooper though, he's going all day, it's like he can feel his master's urgency, and then:

Rufus stops, he's thrown a shoe, the same one he had the blacksmith fix at Hank Cooper's ranch. Colt dismounts and leads him, ever so slowly, toward the lights in the distance. It's a town, a small one, but even a small town has to have a blacksmith. Colt realizes this is futile, he'll never make it by horseback in time, there's only one way to make it home fast enough, and that's by train. Where can he catch a train, and how far is it to get there? It's well after midnight when he reaches Potts Creek, it's day nineteen.

There's a saloon, maybe he can get some information, and some food would be nice. He enters BIG MARY'S PLACE and gets a beer in an almost empty saloon. There's an older, rather large, woman tending bar and a couple of cowboys drinking at a table across the room. He assumes the bartender is Big Mary.

Colt notices one of the cowboys is looking over at him and chatting with the other cowboy he's sitting with. He figures he better get his information and find a place to wait till morning. Before he can get the woman's attention, the cowboy who was looking, comes over to the bar and is whispering to the woman. It's obvious they're talking about him by the way she's glancing his way while the cowboy whispers something to her. The cowboy returns to his table, the woman comes down to talk to Colt:

"Traveling a little late this evening cowboy?" "Yes, ma'am, just passing through, but my horse threw a shoe, is there a blacksmith in town?" "Charlie Peterman is a good blacksmith, won't be in till about seven or so in the morning. What's your name cowboy, I think I may have seen you, maybe in Wichita?" "You may not have seen me before, Ma'am, but something tells me you know who I am."

She smiles, "Are you Maggie's friend, Colt McCoy?" "Yes Ma'am, you knew Maggie?" "My name is Mary, they call me Big Mary, I own this place, Maggie and I worked together for a while a few years back, she was a good woman. That cowboy over there, was there the night you shot one of Maggie's killers, he recognized you when you came in."

Colt and Mary talk for a while and he tells her about his problem with Rufus and needing to catch a train. She immediately started helping: "Hey, Zeke, as soon as Charlie opens, take this man's horse over there. Tell him he threw a shoe and to take real good care of him." "Thank you, Mary, I appreciate your help," says Colt, "And I'm sorry about Maggie, I feel like it was my fault."

"One thing about Maggie, she was a good judge of character, if you were her friend, you must be a good guy." "I don't know about that, but I thank you Mary." "Now, about you needing to catch a train south, there should be one the day after tomorrow. About a mile from here, there's a sharp turn in the tracks, where they have to slow down. If you stand there with a ten-dollar bill in the air, they will let you jump on board. You still have to buy a ticket but at least you're on board."

"Mary, about Rufus, my horse, could you do me a favor?" Mary listens for a minute, "I'll be glad to take care of Rufus for you. Now, come on and I'll get you something to eat, you can sleep upstairs. By the way, Colt McCoy, no one will bother you in Big Mary's Place or they'll have to deal with Big Mary."

Colt rests for most of the next day, he goes to check on Rufus, he's been a good friend. Colt is very sad because he knows he probably won't see him again. He stays at the livery for quite a while, he hates to leave, it's funny how you can get attached to an animal. Rufus, can sense something, maybe the emotion from his master, his friend, and is very fidgety. Colt, hugs his friend, they've been together for so long, the last two years has been the two of them alone.

Mary has arranged for Zeke to drive Colt to where the train slows down. He has a hard time leaving Rufus, there's no other way, he has to go, with one last hug and one last good-bye, Colt walks out not looking back. This journey he's been on has cost him a lot, now it's cost him Rufus.

Colt waits by the sharp bend in the railroad tracks, he soon hears the train approaching. He does like Mary said and holds up a ten-dollar bill, he sees there's only two passenger cars, the rest are empty cattle cars being moved to the next stop to be filled with cattle. The train slows, the Engineer leans out and takes the money from Colt's hand and tells him to jump on board. Colt grabs hold of the first passenger car's hand rail and pulls himself up.

The train is slowly taking the long sharp curve as Colt enters the car. It's pretty crowded so Colt is about to sit in the first seat when he sees a waving hand, it's Jesse Harris. Jesse is sitting by the window and one of his traveling buddy's is asleep beside him, so Jesse can't get up. Colt waves back and Jesse gestures like he'll be up there to see Colt when he can.

As Colt is about to sit down, he sees another familiar face, who doesn't see him, it's the cowboy who was with Todd Mooney when he killed Maggie. He's sitting in the back and he looks pretty nervous. Colt sits down quickly so not to be seen, he remembered what Jesse had said, about there's going to be a lot of money on the train, because of the cattle sold by him and his traveling partners. He's guessing Todd Mooney may be in the other passenger car and he and his pals are going to rob the train. Why else would the cowboy be on a south bound train?

Colt lays back like he's asleep, pulling his hat down over his face, he takes the dime store novel out of his saddle bags and lays it on his lap. Right here would be a good place for Mooney and his gang to try something before the train can get back up to speed. Sure enough, the train comes to a screeching halt.

The Cowboy, and one of his friends, stand up: "DON'T

NOBODY MAKE ANY FAST MOVES AND NOBODY WILL GET HURT," says the cowboy, his guns are drawn. The door to the car opens and Todd Mooney comes in with a shotgun ready to fire, he stands just inside the door. This car is where the money is, it's where Jesse and his friends are. There's no way to do this, Colt thinks, he can't shoot the three of them fast enough because they're in a straight line. He can, get the first two, but Mooney will get him with the shotgun. He has no choice, it's going to take something special, he has to try, he waits.

The cowboy who helped kill Maggie is coming up the aisle first, the other cowboy holds a bag, and follows, "PUT EVERYTHING IN THE BAG, DON'T MAKE US KILL YOU OVER A FEW DOLLARS. PUT IT ALL IN THERE, AND HURRY UP." Jesse and his friend's hand over thousands of dollars. But the cowboys want everything, the cowboy is nearing Colt, Colt pretends to be asleep. The cowboy kicks Colts feet, "Wake up, and hand it over."

Colt looks up at the cowboy, the cowboy sees Colt, a look of fear is on his face," You should have gone home to Missouri," Colt says as he fires his gun that he had hidden under the dime store novel and shoots the cowboy, dead, point blank. Colt stands up and shoots the next cowboy in the chest, he staggers backwards, now he has but one shot or die:

Colt shoots immediately, the bullet actually takes off the second cowboy's ear as he is falling to the floor, Mooney is about to shoot, another shot rings out and breaks the glass in the door, as Colt's bullet hits Mooney right between the eyes, he falls back into the door, breaking the rest of the glass, and then to the floor.

Colt looks to see that it was Jesse who had shot the glass out of the door. He also hears more shots outside of the train as Todd Mooney's friend who was holding the horses is shot by the Engineer and the Brakeman. "What a shot, you were quicker than a rattlesnake boy," one of the passengers says to Jesse.

"What? No I......" Jesse tries to explain. The passengers and Jesse's friends will hear nothing of it, "That was magnificent, you know who you just killed? That was Todd Mooney, you just killed Todd Mooney." "That was some fast shootin I tell ya, right between the eyes," says another passenger. "No, wait," says Jesse, but it's too late, he can't stop it now. Jesse looks at Colt with a look of shock on his face but Colt can't help him now. He could try but no one would believe it.

"Thank you, Jesse, we all would have gone broke if you didn't kill that murdering scum," says one of the men traveling with Jesse. "Son, you let me know if you need anything, anything at all, nothing's too good for the man who killed Todd Mooney," says the conductor.

Jesse is still looking at Colt, he's horrified at what's happening, people are shaking his hand and bragging about his shooting, what they're saying isn't true: "You were cool and calm, Jesse, I've never seen anyone stand up to a shotgun like that with a six gun." "No I wa.... ."

"Now, don't be modest, you're going to be famous, you're the man that killed Todd Mooney." Jesse sits down, he didn't do anything, it was Colt that made a shot maybe one in ten thousand men could make. Maybe even one in a hundred thousand, he can't shoot, he missed from ten feet away, he wasn't calm, he was terrified. What will happen now? The train is moving again.

The train stops in the morning to drop off the empty cattle cars, people get off the train to get a quick bite to eat and the first thing they do is start telling people about Jesse Harris, the man who shot Todd Mooney. "Drop that shotgun or I'll drop you Mooney. Jesse gave him warning enough." Colt hears one man telling the story to a newspaper man who's writing it down as fast as the man can tell it. And so it begins for Jesse. Jesse doesn't get off the train, he stares out the window. The train is soon moving again, it can make good time now that it's dropped the cattle cars. They will be in Oklahoma sometime tomorrow. At each stop it's the same, news travels fast.

Colt is excited to know he'll be in Deepwater in a few hours, it's been a long ride on the train, but it's good to know he'll see his family soon. He also wants to see Kay, but then a thought comes to mind, what will Mike say about him seeing her? He doesn't want to draw against Mike, he certainly, doesn't want to kill Mike. He wouldn't blame him for being upset, but he needs to see her, he wants to see her, he's going to, nobody's going to stop him, nobody.

The train pulls into the station at Deepwater, he's home, he'll rent a horse from the livery stable and go to the ranch. But to his surprise, he doesn't go straight home, he stops by the meadow, there's a frame of a house being built, Ethan and June's. He stops at the hickory tree, and for old time's sake, he draws, and shoots a couple of rounds into the tree. A lot has happened since he did that for the first time, if he'd only known?

Seeing the family, and now the girls too, was even better than he imagined. He hugged his mom, she didn't want to let go, her baby was home. The dinner was the best he's had in two years as they sat around the table and talked. "Colt, we want you to know if this baby is a boy, we're going to call him C. J. for Colt Junior," says June.

Colt doesn't know what to say, he gets up and hugs June and Ethan. They talk for hours as Colt tells them the whole story of his two-year journey. Mark offers to go get Rufus but Colt tells him it won't be necessary. Colt rides to the oak grove as the sun comes up, he'll wait there all day if he has to. She knows, he's home, Jesse has told her, he'll wait. But as he approaches the grove he sees a buggy already there, it's her, it's Kay.

He jumps off his horse and runs to her, they hug so tightly, she feels so soft and warm. He has thought about her so much and it feels good to know she's here, he wants her to be happy. "Oh, Colt, I've worried so much about you, I didn't know if you were alive or dead. I've read that stupid dime store novel a hundred times. I've missed you, so much."

"I'm sorry Kay, for all of this, I've thought about it, dreamed about it, what I should have done, could have done. What our lives could have been if all this never happened. I'm sorry for hurting you, I just couldn't come home, until now." "What happens now Colt? You know I'm engaged to Mike, but I'll.... ..." Kay begins to cry.

Colt holds her tight and whispers in her ear, he wants to make sure she's alright, he's risked it all to come here for this moment. He needs her to be ok, no matter what the cost, he'll pay it. They talk for a long while, he has so much to tell her, he needs, down deep in his soul, for her to be happy. The tears run down her face and onto his shirt, please be ok, please........ .

Colt stands outside of his home with his family, they're getting ready to go to church, the girls look so pretty and happy. Colt hugs each of his family one by one, he's missed them all and it feels good to be home, if only for a little while. Colt rides with his mother in one buggy, the girls ride with his father in another, the boys follow behind.

Colt sits with his mother in the pew, it feels normal, this is how it was meant to be. He looks over at Ethan, sitting with June and her family, June looks so pretty. The girls sit on the other side of his father with Mark, he notices the girls are holding hands, he's happy for them.

Then he turns his head slowly to the left, until he can see, until he can see Kay, she's looking, just as he expected, she's trying to smile, but it looks like she's holding back tears, Colt understands. His mother takes his hand and holds it throughout the service.

When the service is over Colt leaves the church, he stands on the top step of the church and takes a look around, there's a lot of memory's here, he grew up here. He walks slowly down the walkway, to the buggy, he climbs up on the buggy and is standing. He looks back and can see his parents talking to the preacher. Ethan is helping June down the steps and Jesse comes over to help also.

Colt looks down the road and can see a lone rider sitting on a big horse, the rider reaches for his rifle, and starts to remove it from the case hanging on the side of his horse. Colt turns his head slowly to see his mother, then turns back to the rider who is now aiming his rifle at Colt. Smoke goes up from the rifle, and then the loud CRACK, can be heard.

Colt grabs his chest and it's like he's falling backwards in slow motion, until he hits the cold hard ground. He's lying there on the ground, he looks up at the blue sky above, he thinks of all the people he met, those he hoped he was able to help, it went by so slowly at the time, but now it seems it went by so fast, and now.

He thinks of her in that orange dress, and how soft her lips were the first time they kissed. He lays his head back in the soft grass, "Dear God, let it end." Ethan and Mark come running through the crowd, "LET US THROUGH, LET US THROUGH," Ethan kneels down beside his brother, Mark lays his head on the buggy and starts to cry.

"COLT, NO, NO COLT, NOT THIS WAY, DEAR GOD, NO...." it's Kay. She buries her face in Mike's chest. Ethan stands, removes his coat, and lays it over Colt's face. He turns and finds June standing near-by, they hug and June also begins to cry. "He went that way," someone says pointing the way of the lone rider. "LET HIM GO," says Colt's father, we don't want to know, no one needs to know, who, let it all end here." No one moves.

Jesse and his brothers come over to Ethan, "We'd be honored if you would allow us to dig the grave, maybe in the oak grove?" "Thank you, but not there," says Ethan," It began at the old hickory tree, that's where it will end, we'll bury him there."

Colt's mom stands on the front step of the church being comforted by the preacher. "Better it ends here, rather than laying on some dirty saloon floor, or shot in the back again," says the preacher softly to Kattie McCoy. She watches as Ethan and Mark place Colt's body in the rear of the buggy. Someone hands them a blanket, they cover him, then the family takes Colt home......

A wagon turns slowly into the meadow, in the back is a casket made of hickory wood. There's a crowd, some are strangers to each other, yet tied together in a way they may never know. Hank Cooper, Roy and Rudy from the Bar C Ranch, Jed Lane, and there is a young man, nicely dressed, almost un-recognizable, Luke Parker, standing with his brother Henry.

Kay was there too, crying softly, standing with her father and four brothers. Everyone was here that was supposed to be here, it's over now. No more aimless traveling, no more strangers following, no more shots on a rainy night, no more dreams. Mike gets down from the wagon and the Harris boys, Roy and Luke Parker carry the casket to the grave. The preacher begins, "The Lord is my shepard......"

When the preaching is over, it's Hank Cooper and Henry Parker who shovel the dirt onto the casket. Marshall John stops to pay his respects to Colt's parents, "I don't think anyone knew it would end like this, but it's over now, I'm sorry it had to be this way, but better here now, like this, then to be gunned down like an animal on some lonesome road and you never would know. I'm so sorry."

"Our lives are changed forever, we thank you for letting us be here today," says Luke Parker, he and Henry, as well as the others leave the family to grieve. The family gathers to-gether, alone now, it's over........

Chapter Eight

LADY ON A TRAIN

She looks out the window of the train at the darkening sky. Rain begins to fall against the window but she hardly notices. She's thinking of all that's happened and all the lives that have been changed. It's over now for good, Colt McCoy is but a legend, and the legend grows. She has on her lap a copy of the latest dime store novel, ASSASSIN'S BULLET. She's read it over and over and knows he will live on as long as young boys are fascinated by a fast gun. Colt may have been the fastest gun alive, but it came at a high price.

She had to leave home, it was the only way, she had thought about it ever since he left. Things would be different for her too, there was a price she too must pay. If loving him came at a cost, so be it, she had no control over her heart, the heart wants what the heart wants.

The train rolls into the dark rainy night, she stares into the dark through a, rain stained, window. She closes her eyes and thinks of him, their time together, she loves him more than words could ever express, and that will never end. The train pulls into the station a little after daylight," Fifteen minutes," calls out the conductor, "Just long enough to take on water."

She stays in her seat and soon sees a young man board the train. He comes over and sits down beside her, he takes her into his arms and they share a long kiss that was a long time coming: "I've thought about you, ever since I left, I dreamed about you and only you, from the moment we parted. I want you to know it's you I need, you I want," he whispers so softly to her.

"I've missed you so much and hoped you would come back to me," they share another long kiss, "I didn't want to live my life without you, I knew it from the start," she says. "I love you, Colt." "I love you too, Dianna"

"I had to go home and make sure Kay was alright, I hoped you'd understand. When Jesse told me she was crying in the oak grove a month before, I knew I had to go home and let her know it was alright to move on with Mike. What we had was an opportunity lost in the past, as big of a shame that it is, it was time to let it go. I wanted her to know it was alright to do that. Besides, I had to go home to bring this to an end."

He had come up with the idea when Luke Parker had told him the story about him killing Colt. He thought, what if the lie became the truth, or in this case, what if the lie became another lie? There were a lot of people who had to help, but it went off, perfectly.

"You know what makes me happy?" Dianna asks, "I'm glad Pops is a good enough shot to have missed you there at the church," they both laugh. "I'm sure Danny will take good care of Rufus too," Colt takes Dianna into his arms, this is no dream, this is real.

In the rear of the passenger car is Mr. Cooper, Rudy and Roy, riding back home, "My shoulder is killing me," says Roy. "From what?" asks Rudy. "That darned casket, it was heavy," says Roy. "Heavy as a box of rocks, wasn't it?" says Coop, they all laugh and are so happy for the young couple in front of them.

THE END?